A DEATH IN DIDLINTON

A suspicious death — and a gorgeous new neighbour — are not exactly what Poppy was expecting when she arrives at her usual holiday cottage by the sea! Drawn into solving the mystery with the attractive Simon by her side, Poppy discovers intrigue and danger in sleepy Didlinton, which draw ever closer the more she investigates. With not only her estranged mother arriving unexpectedly, but also Simon's ex-girlfriend turning up to cause trouble, will Poppy manage to both solve the case and find love?

CAROL MacLEAN

A DEATH IN DIDLINTON

Complete and Unabridged

LINFORD
Leicester

First published in Great Britain in 2021

First Linford Edition
published 2022

A catalogue record for this book is available
from the British Library.

ISBN 978–1–4448–4952–3

1

The phone rang just as Poppy Johnson was sitting on her suitcase, endeavouring to get the zip to close.

She was expecting the call — but not the message it contained. A message which, although she didn't yet know it, was going to make for an exciting and dangerous summer.

School had finished for the summer holidays and Poppy had said goodbye to thirty very happy eight-year-olds, tidied her classroom and shut its door with a sigh of contentment and anticipation.

Now, she was in her Edinburgh flat, getting ready for her annual trip south to Didlinton-by-the-Sea. She always spent the six-week holiday at her Aunt Gilly's cottage, house-sitting and cat-sitting while her aunt travelled abroad.

Aunt Gilly always called at five o'clock on the day school finished up. This was to give Poppy any last minute instructions, because she was usually abroad by the time Poppy arrived at the cottage.

It was an arrangement that suited them both. Gilly would arrive back a week before Poppy left for Edinburgh and her job, and they then spent those days catching up and telling each other about their respective vacations.

'Hello, Poppy here.' She stood up with a smile.

'Hello, Poppy there. Are you packed? Have you remembered your umbrella this year? We're getting lovely weather right now — but then again, last summer started off well and look where that ended up.'

'I didn't remember my umbrella,' Poppy said, staring at the suitcase top which had sprung open and released some tops and skirts from their prison. 'I'm not sure I've got room for an umbrella. I'll just have to take my chances and hope the sun stays out.'

'It's all fluffy white clouds and blue skies and little sailing boats down here,' her aunt said cheerfully. 'Now, I'll be on the ferry to France tonight so I won't see you but I've left some bread and milk and jam, that sort of thing, for you.'

'Thanks, but you shouldn't have. I can go to the village shop when I get there.'

They had the same conversation every year. It was a bit of a ritual and Poppy knew that Gilly liked to leave supplies despite Poppy's protests.

'How are the cats?' she asked.

The cats got lonely on their own in the cottage, according to Gilly, and they were half of the reason for Poppy going down. Of course, having someone live in the cottage in case of burglars was comforting too. It meant Gilly could enjoy her five weeks abroad without worrying, and Poppy had a holiday home rent-free.

'Ah, well, that's one of the things I wanted to mention to you. Bubbles and Geoffrey are in fighting form, literally. You'll see Bubbles has a torn ear, but it's mending nicely so you don't have to do anything.

'But little Delilah isn't well, poor thing.

I don't want to leave her, but my trip is all booked. So I hope you'll take great care of her.'

'What's the matter with her?' Poppy felt a little tremor of dread. What if something happened to Gilly's precious youngest feline while she was away? It didn't bear thinking about.

'I don't know. She's just being . . . odd. Sniffing in corners, being secretive and eating a lot, but scrawny round the haunches. What do you think?'

'Me? I wouldn't have a clue.'

'Anyway, I've dewormed them all as a precaution. That's probably the cause. If you can give her extra cuddles, I'd be glad. She misses me. They all do when I'm away.'

'I will do,' Poppy promised, thinking privately that the cats seemed perfectly happy as long as they had food and a warm spot to sleep. In her experience they didn't appear to pine for their owner at all over the holidays.

'Oh, I almost forgot. How dreadful of me. It's about Her Next Door.'

4

Aunt Gilly lived in a row of tiny cottages near the seaside. One on side lived Harry Beveridge, who was in his eighties and still went for a bracing sea swim every morning, pruned Gilly's privet hedge for her and did various other odd jobs around the place as the need arose.

On the other side was Her Next Door, as Gilly referred to her other neighbour. They didn't get along. Her Next Door was a woman in her sixties who objected to Gilly's cats using her garden for nefarious purposes. They had had a nasty argument about the matter ten years before and had never really spoken to each other since. In fact, Poppy didn't even know the woman's proper name.

'What's happened?' Poppy asked, wondering whether she, in fact, even needed to know.

'She's dead. Fell off a cliff in the hills behind the village. The police are calling it an accident. I can't say I liked the woman but it's simply awful. Especially when she'd just had good news. Oh well, we don't know what's round the corner, any one of us, do we?'

'That's terrible. It must have been a shock to everyone. Did she have any family?'

'There was a sister, I believe. Harry knows more than I do. You mustn't let it bother you, though. Perhaps I shouldn't have mentioned it, only it's the talk of the village so you'd find out when you come down. Better to hear it from me, I expect. Now, I must dash and get ready for my travels. Do enjoy yourself this summer, my dear. I'll send you a postcard.'

The phone went down in Didlinton and Poppy was left staring at her blank screen.

Before long, doing battle with her suitcase, she forgot about her aunt's news.

* * *

Over the next couple of days she was busy with her long train journeys and after too many railway sandwiches and watery coffees, and a night in a noisy, cheap hotel, she was dragging her suitcase off the train and breathing in the lovely sea air.

The salty tang of the sea and the roar of the waves on the beach brought back a myriad of memories from the years she'd been visiting Aunt Gilly. It had begun her first year out of teaching college and fresh into her first full-time teaching job. She hadn't had any money to go travelling and when Gilly offered her the cottage, Poppy had jumped at the opportunity.

The following year, she had been too busy to make travel plans and so it was convenient to accept the offer once again. After that, it seemed natural to go there, and now it was a comfortable tradition and a happy place to be. She'd rather be in Gilly's snug little cottage only a single cobbled street away from the beach, than backpacking round Europe the way some of her friends did.

She had brought Alex with her last year, but he hadn't liked it. They had split up and he'd gone back to Edinburgh. Oddly, the split hadn't caused her as much pain as she'd thought, and being in the cottage had healed her very quickly.

This year, there was no significant other to worry about. She was free to enjoy paddling in the sea, feeling the sand under her bare toes and taking breakfast at Katie's Diner on the promenade every day if she chose to.

She arrived at Gilly's cottage out of breath from pulling the heavy suitcase. Maybe she'd brought too much clothing after all. It was a balmy summer's evening, the sun still high in the sky and a warm breeze coming from the beach bringing the sound of children's laughter and the cry of the gulls.

The key was under the ceramic toadstool to the side of the path. She took it, opened the cottage door and stepped inside. There was a scent of lavender and beeswax. Gilly had left a vase of lavender sprigs on the dresser in the hall. Poppy touched them, smiling at the thoughtful touch.

Next to the vase was a piece of white

paper. Gilly had scribbled *Have fun!* on it.

The hallway was tiny. She had to slide past the old dresser to get to the kitchen. On the table there, she found a plate with a paper doily and a selection of small pots of home-made jam, a loaf of bread and a tub of brownies. She checked the fridge. Gilly had stocked it with milk, butter, eggs and an enormous lettuce.

Back in the hall, the other door led to a small living room with mismatched furniture and a large flatscreen television. Gilly might love the country life but she wouldn't miss her soaps for anything. Especially *Heaven's Harvest*, a soap which was filmed right here in Didlinton-by-the-Sea. Gilly had even appeared in one episode, walking past with her shopping bag in the background, without knowing she was being filmed.

Poppy climbed the narrow staircase, dragging her suitcase up, bump bump behind her. Up here there was one main bedroom, a tiny second bedroom and a bathroom, both with sloping ceilings on which she had often banged her head in her early visits.

The bed had been made up for her in the main bedroom with a gold-wrapped chocolate left on the pillow. This was Aunt Gilly's little joke, as if Poppy had come to stay at a grand hotel. It was always the same brand of chocolate, her aunt's favourite.

She unwrapped it and popped it into her mouth as she wondered whether she should hang her clothes in the wardrobe. She decided she'd do it later.

There was a knock at the door downstairs. She clattered down, but the door opened before she got there and Harry walked in.

'Hello, thought it was you. How are the bonny Highlands? All white heather and bagpipes, I imagine. I brought you this. Caught it myself this afternoon.'

He waggled a large fish by its tail and grinned, showing his missing teeth. Harry had a piratical air — he only needed a black eye patch and a beard to truly look the part.

'Thanks very much,' Poppy said weakly. 'I was going to buy fish and chips for my dinner.'

'You won't have to now,' Harry said cheerfully, 'Just put this chappie under the grill and it'll be much tastier. You'll have to gut it first, of course — but I'm sure you'll manage that, you being a teacher and all.'

'Right,' she agreed, wondering whether there was a YouTube video on gutting fish that she could watch later.

'I'll put it in the sink for you.'

She followed him back into the kitchen.

'How are you, Harry? You look well,' she said.

'I'm fit as a proverbial flea, my love. Not much to tell. Didlinton is same as always. The television bods are back filming the next series. My sister, Dottie, has had her hip done and my grandson's wife has just produced her second bouncing baby.'

He leaned in, suddenly serious. 'Did Gilly tell you about Mary Soull?'

'Is that the lady who lived next door?'

'That's right. Terrible tragedy.'

There was a gleam in Harry's eye which Poppy ignored. Harry was an inveterate gossip and even the untimely end of Her Next Door was fair game, it seemed.

'The police say it was an accident. The case is closed and the funeral was last week.'

He shook his head darkly.

'What? Surely if the police say that, it must be true.'

Poppy felt like shaking her own head. Was Harry simply making mischief? Maybe there wasn't enough gossip in Didlinton and he was stirring for more.

'Fit as a fiddle, that woman and as nimble as a mountain goat. Fall off a cliff? Mary? Highly unlikely, if you ask me. Which they haven't, as it turns out. If the police had bothered to speak to the village, they might have found out more. That's all I'll say on the subject.'

Poppy stifled a yawn politely. The travelling and the exhaustion of a term's teaching was beginning to creep up on her. She longed for her dinner and a strong cup of coffee, and then to tuck her feet up under her and watch a movie on Gilly's enormous television.

'You're half asleep and here's me rattling on, you should've told me to shut up,' Harry said, putting a large paw on her shoulder and patting it. 'I'll leave you to it. I put a lettuce in the fridge, it's one of mine fresh from the soil.'

'Thanks, Harry. You're very kind,' Poppy said and kissed his weathered cheek.

'You know where I am if you need me,' Harry said gruffly, hiding his pleasure. He touched his fingers to his brow in salute and headed out, sliding past the dresser with the skill of years of practice.

Poppy stared at the fish in the sink. It stared back with one unwinking round eye. She left it there and instead cut herself some bread and spread it with butter and jam. There was a bag of coffee in the cupboard above the ancient stove and she made some up.

She sat with her impromptu meal,

wondering what was missing. After a while, she realised it was the cats. The cottage was empty except for her. She left her plate and cup on the draining board, unable to wash them because of Harry's fish. She peered out the window into the back garden. It was a lovely evening so she expected that Bubbles, Geoffrey and Delilah were outside sunning themselves.

She went outside into the neat garden. There was a small patio with garden furniture — two wrought iron chairs and a table, a well-kept lawn and flower-filled borders. There were hollyhocks, delphiniums, marigolds and all sorts of other colourful flowers and plenty of bees too.

Bubbles, a fluffy ginger cat, was lying in the back flower bed, crushing some plants. Polly noted his ragged ear. He blinked at her with yellow eyes but didn't bother to get up and greet her. Something touched her bare ankles and she jumped.

It was Geoffrey, always the most affectionate of Gilly's cats. He was a black and white short-haired moggy. She picked him up.

'Hello, Geoffrey, how are you? It's been a long while since we saw each other, hasn't it?'

Geoffrey agreed by pushing his nose into her hand and purring.

'Where's Delilah? I'd really like to find her because Gilly's quite concerned about her.'

If Geoffrey knew, he wasn't telling. Poppy put him down and he stretched out on the warm paving stones and rolled about.

It was possible that Delilah was next door in Mary Soull's garden. After all, that was the reason for the argument all those years ago — even if, in those days, it had been a different set of Gilly's cats. Even now, Delilah could be digging holes in next door's flowerbeds.

Poppy glanced over the low hedge. There was no sign of anyone. Of course there wasn't. Poor Mary Soull was gone. No one would mind, would they, if Poppy slipped into next door's garden to look for a small, bony grey cat?

She went round the side of Gilly's cottage and let herself in through the gate of the cottage beside it. She didn't bother to knock on the front door. It was empty, after all.

She went straight down the side path and into the back garden. The lawn here was growing straggly. The flowerbeds needed weeding and a large butterfly bush had got well out of control.

Something moved under the butterfly bush. Poppy ducked down to see a grey tail twitching.

'Delilah, there you are. Come on out, this isn't your garden. Although there's no one here to tell you off now that Ms Soull's had her accident. Or otherwise. Here, kitty, kitty. Oh, for goodness' sake, Delilah, get out here or I'll pull you out.'

The cat didn't budge but stared at her sullenly. Poppy knelt down and crawled under the butterfly bush. She tried to get her hands round Delilah but the cat slithered backwards, even further into the undergrowth.

At that moment, she heard a noise behind her. She froze, unable to turn easily to see who or what it was.

'Put your hands up and come out where I can see you.' A man's voice said.

'I can't put my hands up,' Poppy said, 'I need them to get out of here.'

There was a silence before he spoke again. 'OK, just . . . just come out here and no nonsense.'

The butterfly bush caught her hair and she shrieked. Then she slid out, her hair over her face, dusty earth and leaf debris all over her skirt and blouse. When she pushed her hair out of her eyes, she saw a tall man standing there with a rolling pin upraised in one hand.

'Are you seriously going to hit me with that?' she said.

'No. No, I was . . . baking.' He lowered the rolling pin, looking embarrassed.

Poppy noticed he was around the same age as her and that he was really very attractive with brown hair, blue eyes and the sort of strong jaw that women dream about in a man.

'Look I'm sorry, I didn't think anyone was here,' she said, 'I just came to get Delilah.'

'Who's Delilah?' He was still tense-looking as if he thought she was lying. The rolling pin was clutched in his hand like a weapon.

'She's my aunt's cat. I'm Poppy, I'm house-sitting next door.'

'Simon Carruthers, I'm house-sitting too, in a way. My aunt died recently and I've inherited her cottage apparently.'

He smiled and Poppy's heart thumped unexpectedly. It was a lovely smile, showing even white teeth and creating a small but definite dimple in his right cheek. She smiled back.

'Were you really baking?'

He looked at the rolling pin and then at her. 'No, I wasn't baking. That was a lie. I thought you were an intruder so I armed myself with the nearest thing and it happened to be a rolling pin.'

'It's not bad,' Poppy said, 'You could do some real damage with that.'

He shuddered. 'Don't say that. What

if I'd brained you one? How awful. I'd never forgive myself.'

'Well, you didn't, so cheer up. It's my fault for trespassing. I'll go home now and leave you to whatever you were doing.'

'What about Delilah?' He frowned.

Poppy knelt down and had a good look under the shrubs.

'I'm pretty sure she's gone.'

She stood up and brushed more dust off her skirt.

Simon hesitated. 'Would you like a coffee?'

2

'You do realise they were sworn ene-
mies?' Poppy said, gratefully watching
Simon gut the fish.

She poured the coffee he'd made into
two china cups. He had turned on the
grill and produced a pat of butter from
his fridge. Poppy had brought the lettuce
too, and Simon had found four tomatoes
to make up a salad. It had been only fair,
she thought, to share her supper after he
invited her for coffee. The bread and jam
hadn't been enough to fill her up.

Besides, he was clearly an expert at
dealing with a dead fish. Her sink was
free of the beast and she wouldn't have
to lie to Harry when he asked her if she'd
enjoyed eating it.

'Who were?' Simon asked, sounding
slightly distracted as he removed the spi-
nal column.

Poppy screwed up her eyes and looked
away.

'Your aunt and mine. Didn't she mention that?'

'I didn't actually know her that well,' he said, laying thick fillets on the grill and adding curls of butter. 'Would you mind cutting up the salad?'

'Oh, sorry.' Poppy grabbed the knife he'd left for her and began chopping.

There were a few moments of silence while the meal was prepared. The late evening sunshine streamed in the kitchen window, the colour of old gold. Glancing about, Poppy thought how different Mary Soull's cottage was compared to Gilly's, despite the same architectural layout. While Gilly's home was packed with odd pieces of furniture and stacked with books and cushions, pot plants and ornaments, Mary Soull's home was colour co-ordinated with matching, quality furniture which looked quite new. None of it was scuffed. Of course, there were no cats living here, which helped.

There were a number of framed photographs and paintings of birds on the cream-painted walls, and a pair of binoculars lay on top of a book shelf.

'So what was the feud about?' Simon asked, finally, sliding the cooked fish onto plates and placing them on the kitchen table.

Poppy added the bowl of salad to the table and sat opposite him.

'Gilly's cats and their rude ways in the garden.'

'Ahh. I can see why that might be annoying. It looks as if my aunt was very tidy. Although, the grass does need mowing. That'll be tomorrow's task.'

'Did you really not know her at all?' Poppy asked. *And if so, why did she leave you her home?*

'The inheritance came out of the blue. I arrived last week for the funeral and was surprised to find nothing had been touched. It looks like no one has been in here since the day of her ... demise.'

'Gilly said something about there being a sister?'

'Yes, that's my Mum. But she and Mary didn't get on. I think Mary left me the cottage as a snub to Mum, to be honest.'

'Oh dear. Do you know what you're going to do with it?'

'I've got the summer to decide. I'm between jobs right now, so I'm going to live here for the next couple of months and then I'll see.'

Poppy felt a little rush of pleasure that he'd be there all summer. Only because he was good company. That was all. It was nice to find a friend, just next door. It was nothing to do with his dimple or the colour of his eyes which were just the shade of the afternoon sea.

'What do you do for a living?' she asked.

'I'm a teacher. I was teaching at a boys' school in the north-east but my contract finished up and although they asked me to stay on, I feel as if I need to spread my wings a bit. What about you?'

'I'm a teacher too.' Poppy smiled. 'I teach primary three and absolutely love it. Mind you, I love the holidays too. It can be exhausting.'

Their talk turned to teaching, and how demanding but satisfying it was to educate young minds. It wasn't until they had scraped the remains of their dinner into the food recycling bin and topped up their coffees that Simon spoke again about his aunt.

Poppy was thinking that it was getting late and she was probably wearing out her welcome.

'I should get going,' she said, standing up reluctantly.

'My mother thinks it's suspicious,' Simon blurted out.

Poppy sank back into her chair.

'What do you mean?'

Simon shook his head. 'My aunt's death. She thinks it's odd.'

'So . . . you think she . . . what? Had a heart attack or a stroke and toppled off the cliff?'

Poppy tried to remember how old Simon's aunt was. What had Gilly told her? She was in her sixties?

'I think Mum wonders if she was murdered.'

His words seemed to echo in the room, with its polished wood floor and spartan wooden blinds.

Poppy blinked. Had she heard right? Simon's face was flushed and his jaw tight.

'Murdered?' she whispered, unwilling to hear the unnerving echo again. Surely he was joking?

He nodded, his face returning to its usual tanned colour. 'Sorry to sound so melodramatic. But, yeah, that's what she thinks.'

'Well.' She breathed in. 'It is quite melodramatic. I thought the police said it was an accident — Gilly told me that.'

'They don't always get it right, you know.'

'No, of course not,' she said hastily. 'But still . . .'

'I'm sorry,' he said, pushing his chair back from the kitchen table. 'It's nothing to do with you. I shouldn't have said anything. I've spoiled the evening. And I was enjoying our dinner together.'

'You haven't spoiled it,' Poppy said,

feeling ridiculously happy that he'd enjoyed her company. 'You can talk to me about it, if you want. What makes your mum think she was murdered?'

Really, she shouldn't encourage talk about such a dreadful topic while her heart was singing merrily. She tried to dampen her spirits by reminding herself of Alex and how that had turned out. It worked to some degree. A bit more sombrely, she repeated her question and tried to focus on how awful it was if it was true.

'She sent a letter to my Mum just before it happened. Although they didn't get on, they kept in touch once or twice a year. Generally cards at Easter and Christmas, that sort of thing. But out of the blue, Mum got a letter in early June. She was so surprised, she told me about it. Turned out that Mary wanted to visit her. She'd fixed on a date in mid-June and had already booked her train tickets. She was like that, apparently. Wouldn't take no for an answer so it hadn't even occurred to her that her little sister, my

Mum, would refuse, that she couldn't come and visit. Not that Mum would. She's so kind and gentle.'

Poppy tried to keep up.

'But she never turned up?' She hazarded a guess.

'Exactly. Mum waited in the car park at the railway station and tried phoning her, but it kept ringing out. Of course, she was dead by then. A man walking a dog found her lying at the bottom of the cliffs.'

'So, the question is, what was she doing walking along the cliffs when she should have been on a train?'

Simon nodded. Then he shrugged and gave a sigh.

'Of course, I've tried telling Mum that it doesn't have to be suspicious. Maybe Aunt Mary simply changed her mind about visiting. She was quite capable of that, and of not bothering to let Mum know until the next day. And then she went out walking and tripped. That's what the police are saying.'

'And what do you think?'

'I don't know. Murder seems too fantastic, like something off the telly. It's more plausible that she tripped and fell. Besides, who'd want to kill her?'

'Can't you leave it at that?'

'I'd like to, believe me,' Simon sighed again. 'But my mother has made me promise to investigate it over the summer. Not through the police, obviously, but to keep my ears and eyes open.'

He stood up and Poppy took that as her cue to leave. She stood too.

'Thanks so much for making dinner,' she said. 'You've saved me from Harry's reproaches if I hadn't eaten that enormous fish.'

Simon laughed. 'Glad to help. It was delicious.'

'Well, I'd best be off.'

* * *

Gilly's cottage was warm and welcoming as she unlocked the front door and went inside. The summer sunshine had lingered and the lavender scent pervaded the hallway. Poppy breathed in deeply and smiled. She felt it was going to be an interesting summer.

She poured herself a glass of water from the kitchen tap and took it into the living room. The sun was low in the sky and a few stars twinkled. She thought about what Simon had said and what his mother believed. It seemed impossible that such a beautiful, quiet little place as Didlinton could be the location for a murder.

Poppy tried to remember Mary Soull. She had hardly ever seen her on her summer holidays. She had a vague recollection of Gilly's neighbour coming and going next door but because of the feud, she had never called out a greeting and Poppy had been warned not to by Gilly.

Because of that, all she could dredge up out of her memory was a vague, shadowy figure who liked hats. She did remember the hats. Straw with stiff flowers, or felt with felt flowers. Even a bowler hat once. What did that mean? Perhaps Mary had a dramatic side to her.

Poppy shook her head. What did it matter? The poor woman was dead, and it had nothing to do with her. She was here to relax, enjoy her summer holiday and look after the cats.

She went and fetched her book, a paperback thriller, and uncorked a bottle of red wine which she found in the cupboard. She took the wine and the tub of brownies through to the living room. Geoffrey jumped up on the couch beside her and began to purr. Poppy snuggled down with a sigh of contentment. This was wonderful. The summer holidays had begun.

★ ★ ★

Later, she dozed and woke with a start. Her book had slipped off her knee onto the floor and she had a crick in her neck. Her empty wine glass stood on the small table beside the couch and accompanying it was Bubbles, staring balefully at her with his pale yellow eyes. His torn ear drooped slightly and he hissed as she sat up.

'What's that for?' Poppy said. Then she realised he was actually staring at Geoffrey who was blissfully unaware, snoring gently on the sofa. Geoffrey, who was perhaps the culprit behind Bubbles' sore ear.

Bubbles jumped down from the table and meowed.

'Are you hungry?'

She hadn't fed the cats. Jumping up guiltily, she went to the kitchen, Bubbles stalking behind her. Delilah was already there, sniffing at her empty plate. She threw Poppy what seemed like a reproachful glance.

'Ok, I'm sorry, I should've fed you all earlier. In my defence, I was awfully tired from my journey. You try travelling by rail for two days and see if you don't fall asleep on the sofa.'

Poppy put out generous chunks of horrible smelling cat food. Bubbles stuck his head in his bowl, gulping it. Delilah delicately nosed it and then padded away. Poppy shook her head. Aunt Gilly was right, Delilah was behaving rather oddly.

She followed the grey cat. Delilah kept stopping to sniff at corners, then she ran lightly up the stairs. Poppy waited a moment, then went up after her, as quietly as possible. At first there was no sight of her. Then, hearing a noise in the bathroom, she looked in to see Delilah in the bath tub, drinking from a small puddle of water that had dripped from the tap.

'You do know there's a perfectly good bowl of fresh water downstairs, next to your delicious dinner?'

There was no explaining cats, she decided. Leaving Delilah to her own devices, Poppy went back downstairs to the cosy living room. She browsed the photographs on the mantelshelf over the fireplace. There were several of herself, at various stages from baby to toddler, then sulky teenager and university graduation. There was a lovely one of Aunt Gilly, somewhere foreign under a mimosa tree laughing, a glittering sea behind her. Another one of Aunt Gilly with a dark-haired bear of a man with his arm around her.

That was Poppy's Uncle Jack, one of the kindest men in the world. He had died five years ago and she knew her aunt still missed him as if it was yesterday. It was part of the reason Gilly was always on the move, keeping busy, keeping her thoughts and emotions at bay.

Poppy's fingers hesitated over the next silver-framed photograph. Finally she picked it up and stared at it. Her mother's smiling face stared back. A young Poppy, aged two or three, leaned against her leg. It had been taken on a good day. The sun was shining and the background was the old Edinburgh house where Poppy had grown up. She remembered that pink climbing rose around the blue front door. Half of the rowan tree was visible, cut off by the edge of the frame. It was in blossom too and so the photo must have been taken in June, she guessed.

She searched her mother's face for a clue of what was to come. But there was nothing. Angela Johnson looked peaceful and contented. Her gaze was on the photographer and her eyes were crinkled in amusement. Was it Poppy's dad who had taken the shot?

She sighed and put the photograph back on the mantelshelf. She had been only five when her mother had left, saying she needed to travel. Her Dad had tried his best to bring her up alone but often Aunt Gilly had come to stay for a few days to help, or Poppy had been sent south to stay with Gilly and Uncle Jack for a week or so in the holidays so that her dad could work.

Every so often, her mother would arrive back and stay for a while. As a child, Poppy had wished so hard each time that her mum would realise she needed them and wouldn't leave again.

Later, the older and wiser Poppy wondered why her dad had let Angela stay with them and finally figured out that he still loved her.

It was a strange upbringing in some ways, but Poppy had always known she was loved. Her dad had been a great parent, and her aunt and uncle had lavished her with love and care too. She didn't feel she had missed out too badly.

A loud yowl from upstairs made her heart thump.

'Delilah?' she called, running to the stairs and taking them two at a time.

At the top, she stopped to catch her breath after the sudden exertion. The grey cat was sitting outside the bedroom door. Delilah was composed as if nothing had happened.

'What are you doing? What was the awful screeching all about?' Poppy said crossly. 'You almost gave me a heart attack.'

Delilah blinked once as if to disagree. Then she stalked off, tail low and bony hips swaying. Muttering under her breath, Poppy went back downstairs once again. She was going to be fit if this kept going on.

Now wide awake, she pushed the curtains aside to see the navy sky. It was a lovely night. On a sudden impulse, she shrugged on her cardigan and opened the front door. A walk would be nice, maybe down to the beach and back. The fresh air would help her sleep.

There was no one about as she crunched along the beach, listening to the waves lap against the sand. It felt very peaceful. The air was cool but not unpleasantly so and she took great sucks of it into her lungs, feeling healthy.

It was a long beach, stretching between two jutting headlands. Didlinton village fronted the strand with its old-fashioned Victorian promenade and pastel-coloured houses and shops.

She didn't reach the far headland before deciding to turn back. Now, suddenly, she felt tired and longed for her bed.

She reached the steps to the promenade from the beach and went up, holding the cold iron hand rail. Then she crossed the main road and headed up a side street. Turning to the right, the row of cottages was visible in the street lights. She wasn't paying much attention to her surroundings, thinking of making cocoa before bed. Then she glanced up, her sixth sense kicking in. That feeling of not being alone.

There was a shadowy figure on the street, outside the yellow circle cast by the street light. She couldn't make out whether it was a man or a woman. In the moment before the person saw her, Poppy had the impression they were staring at the cottages.

Then as she opened her mouth to call out, the figure turned and moved away. Very quickly they were swallowed up by the darkness. She guessed whoever it was had gone beyond the last cottage in the row, and was by now heading up the slope of Penny Road which led to the next layer of houses in the village.

Poppy ran to where the figure had stood. What were they looking for? A chill ran lightly up her spine as she realised her location. She was exactly opposite the middle two cottages in the row. One belonged to Mary Soull — or rather Simon. And the other belonged to Aunt Gilly. The unknown person had been staring right at the two cottages.

She sniffed. There was a faint smell of fruit. Sniffing again, she thought it was watermelon and possibly strawberry. How odd.

Once indoors, Poppy reached for Gilly's set of keys which hung on a wooden hook in the hallway. She locked the front door, and went to check that the kitchen door was secure.

Rattling the door knob, she thought with a pang that it was the first time ever in Gilly's cottage that she felt the need to check security. Often, Gilly left the cottage unlocked when she went shopping. Didlinton was such a safe, small place. Wasn't it?

3

Simon was up early as usual the next morning. He rarely slept beyond seven, even in the holidays. He made himself a breakfast of bacon roll, porridge and black coffee before showering and dressing in casual jeans and an open-necked shirt.

This was one of the many things he loved about being on holiday. No need for a suit and tie which constricted his neck and made him feel uncomfortable. He didn't bother with a shave either. Who cared about a few bristles in this heavenly holiday village?

His thoughts flickered swiftly to his new neighbour. He had liked Poppy immediately. Even dishevelled from emerging under the shrubbery, she was gorgeous. She had thick, auburn hair with springy curls and green eyes like a cat. There was something very cute too, about the sprinkling of freckles across the bridge of her nose and across her cheeks.

She obviously had no idea how attractive she was. Not one of those women who basked in male attention and used it mercilessly to manipulate them.

That, of course, reminded him of Susie. He had had a narrow escape. Their wedding was only a month away when he found out she had been seeing his friend, Adam, while they were engaged. Hurt and angry, he had called the whole engagement off and left his job, unable to bear seeing them together.

The wound was still raw. After all, it was only a matter of months since it had happened. It was one of the reasons he was so glad to escape to Didlinton and hole up in Aunt Mary's cottage.

His cottage. It took a bit of getting used to. He no longer had to rent if he didn't wish to. He was now a property owner.

Sipping his coffee, he glanced around. Mary was clearly a tidy woman and the cottage was beautifully furnished and decorated. It was hard to believe that the property was his.

'Am I going to stay here, though?' he asked himself. 'Simon, Simon, what are you thinking? I really must stop talking to myself.'

He could of course talk to Poppy. She was only next door. But was that a good idea? He might find her attractive, but that didn't mean he was in the market for a new romance. In fact, he was positively not in the market. He was wary after Susie. Once bitten, twice shy and all that.

No, he could become friends with Poppy but that was all he could offer.

He chuckled. He was being rather arrogant. Poppy probably didn't find him attractive anyway. There was nothing special about him. He was Mr Average.

He wandered into the living room, raising his eyebrows at the abundance of bird images on the walls. Aunt Mary had clearly been a bird watcher. He couldn't see the attraction in it. It was a bit like trainspotting. Ticking off unusual birds on a list was a strange hobby.

She had taste, he had to admit. The photos and paintings were well executed. There were various bird ornaments, too. A ceramic duck and a couple of carved wooden swans sat on a bookshelf.

He picked up the binoculars, weighing them in his hand. They felt like good quality. It was odd, living in someone else's home. His mum had offered to come and help sort out Mary's belongings and he had been grateful for that. There was no hurry, he'd told her — but yes, when Dad could spare her, it would be great if she could.

He had inherited not only the cottage but also Mary's savings. It was kind of her, but there was no large sum. He didn't care. He hadn't expected any of this. He had tried to pass it all on to his mother, but she was adamant that she didn't want it.

'Mary had her reasons, I must suppose,' she had said. 'Besides, Dad and I have enough to be comfortable. You enjoy the cottage and whatever she's left you, darling. You deserve it. You work hard in that school and they don't appreciate you.'

He heard the gate creak next door and couldn't help glancing out of the window. He saw Poppy's back, straight and slender, her hair bobbing as she walked away down the street.

He felt oddly disappointed. What had he expected? That she'd turn up in his back garden again, hunting cats? Then he could offer her another coffee and have the pleasure of her company.

'Get on with it. Time for some work,' he told himself with a sigh.

Going through someone else's paperwork felt like snooping. It was sad, too. His aunt's whole life was here. Everything from her bank statements to half-packets of pasta and cans of food in the kitchen cupboards to her clothes and an array of hats in the wardrobe upstairs. A life interrupted.

He tried to imagine how it felt to fall off a cliff and failed. It was too horrific for words. And it *must* have been a terrible accident. What was his mother thinking?

His mobile rang and he fumbled in his jeans pocket to pick up the call.

'Simon, darling?'

'Yes, Mum, it's me. You rang my mobile.'

He tried not to roll his eyes. His parents hadn't quite grasped the notion that a mobile phone was personal and not like the landline where they left voice-mails which sounded like dictated letters starting with 'Dear Simon' and finishing with 'Love from your parents'.

'So?'

There was a pause. Simon waited for a moment and then realised that was it, and his mother was asking a question.

'So . . . what?' he said.

'Oh, for goodness sake, Simon, I do believe you are being deliberately dense! I mean, have you found anything out yet about Mary?'

Simon groaned inwardly. He had hoped his mother had forgotten about her suspicions.

'I haven't had a chance yet,' he said.

'I'm busy tidying the cottage and putting stuff in order.'

'She was very tidy, always was, even as a child so there shouldn't be much to tidy.'

His mother sounded sad and Simon relented.

'I will ask about, I promise. It's just . . . a little far-fetched, don't you think? Murder. The police say it was an accident.'

'They would say that. Saves them time and money. To them she's just a silly old woman who can't walk properly on a cliff path. But my sister was very fit. All that bird watching, she had to be. She walked for miles to see her daft birds.'

Something that sounded horribly like a sob echoed in Simon's ear.

'Are you all right, Mum? Do you want me to come home? It's only a couple of hours' drive up the motorway, I could be there by lunch time.'

He heard her blow her nose and sniff.

'Don't be silly, darling. I've got Dad here. I'm really fine. It's just that I miss her. We weren't close, but she was my only sister.'

'Why weren't you close?' he asked, curiously. He had never dared to ask. Growing up, he'd accepted that Aunt Mary only visited at Christmas and occasionally once in the year apart from that.

'I don't know. We kind of drifted apart after our parents passed. I think they were the glue that kept our family together. Mary, of course, was so much older than me. She was more like a second mother to me, growing up, than a sister. Perhaps she resented that. I'm not sure. Now I'll never know for certain.'

'I didn't see her much but she came across as self-sufficient,' Simon said, choosing his words carefully.

'Oh, yes, she gave that impression but I wonder how true that was. Bird watching is a fairly solitary pastime and that was her passion, but she did have a friend she mentioned. Manda or Moira, I can't remember her name. You could start with her.'

'Start with her?' Simon said, confused.

'To investigate Mary's murder.'

'I hoped you'd given up on that.'

'Given up? We haven't even begun!'

'The thing is, Mum . . . there's no evidence to say that she came to a bad end in that way.'

'Simon,' his mother's voice was suddenly firm, 'Mary was coming to visit me. She had booked her train tickets. There has to be a reason she went onto that cliff path that day instead of going to the train station. There simply has to be. What if someone enticed her there?'

'What if she decided not to visit you and went bird watching instead?' Simon asked, struggling not to argue with his mother.

'Will you please promise me to at least look into it a little bit? Start with Manda or Moira. Find her and ask her about Mary's state of mind. Do it for me, darling. Help me put my mind at rest.'

When she put it like that, Simon couldn't very well say no. He wanted his mother to have peace of mind.

'OK, I'll do it,' he promised. 'I'll find Manda and I'll ask her. After that, can we please put this to rest?'

'That depends on what she says. Phone me back when it's done.'

The connection cut out. Simon stared at his mobile, then shook his head and tucked it back into his jeans pocket. He went through to the kitchen and put the kettle on. Strong, black coffee was called for. Once he'd had a couple of mugs of that, he would find Aunt Mary's bank statements and sort through them.

He would look for this Manda or Moira but not right now. He was convinced more than ever that his mother was clutching at straws. Who in Didlinton would want to murder a middle-aged woman like Mary Soull?

★ ★ ★

Poppy had also risen early that morning. This was mainly because she had forgotten to close her bedroom curtains and so the sunshine had streamed in and warmed her eyelids.

The birdsong hadn't helped either. There was a blackbird out there who led the choir with gusto. She stretched and felt good. She bounded out of bed, suddenly starving.

Sipping her coffee and crunching on a piece of toast and honey, she remembered last night and the mysterious watcher. In the bright light of morning, it seemed ridiculous. Had she imagined the whole thing? Why would anyone be watching the cottages?

She turned to more important matters. Like whether Simon was up and whether their paths would cross today. It would be lovely to have another coffee and chat, and find out more about him. *As a friend, of course,* she hastily added in her mind.

That went without saying. She didn't have to add it as small print every time she thought of him. She was perfectly happy being single. After all, look what a drag Alex had turned out to be. She didn't want that again. Spending time with someone who didn't share her interests and could barely be cheerful — uggh! The thought made her shudder.

When she was ready, Poppy borrowed one of Gilly's hessian shopping bags and went down to the seafront. There was a selection of local shops and she enjoyed the old-fashioned feel of getting her fruit and veg at the grocer's, a chicken at the butcher's and a wholemeal loaf at the baker's. She also found a new shop selling gourmet chocolates and bought two small selection boxes.

Swinging her heavy bag, she headed back to the cottage and put her items away. Then she took one of the chocolate boxes and went round to visit Harry. His cottage door was open and she heard whistling.

'Harry?' she called, before stepping inside.

She knew he wouldn't mind. He was used to Gilly popping round, and Poppy had done so too many a time in the holidays.

Harry's home was as familiar as Gilly's cosy place. The cottages all had the same layout. Harry's narrow hallway was crammed with fishing rods, fishing nets, wellies and books about fishing.

She went through to the kitchen and saw the back door was also open. Harry was in his garden, whistling along to a battered, ancient radio and sewing a piece of tarpaulin.

His face lit up in pleasure at the sight of her. He turned off the radio and stood up.

'Hello, my dear. What a nice surprise. Come to visit an old codger, have you?'

Poppy laughed. 'I brought you these.' She held out the box of chocolates, knowing it was one of Harry's weaknesses.

'Bless you, that's very kind. How about a cup of tea and you can help me eat them?'

He didn't wait for an answer but went inside and flipped the kettle switch.

When the tea was ready, he poured

51

two mugs and brought them out to the table, brushing the tarp aside. He took a while, deliberating over a caramel and a mint chocolate, then pushed the box to Poppy, insisting she join him.

Their chat was general at first. Harry told her about his large family's latest escapades and his fishing, and Poppy told him about her class and her year in Edinburgh.

'Not much happens in Didlinton,' Harry said, taking another chocolate and again pushing the box in Poppy's direction. 'Except, of course, this year has been different.'

'You mean Mary Soull's death?' Poppy said, swallowing a strawberry cream. 'Do you think it was an accident, Harry?'

'The police tell us it was. Who are we to argue with the coppers?'

'But you're not sure,' she pushed him.

'There are rumours in the village.'

'What sort of rumours?' Poppy stopped. 'Sorry, it's none of my business.'

'Don't let that stop you.' Harry chuckled. 'Everyone's got a theory.'

'And what's yours?' she couldn't help asking.

'Poor Mary. It was a tragedy, whatever occurred that day. She and I got along all right. Did you know that? Gilly didn't like her and Mary couldn't stand Gilly. All that business with the cats in her garden. But she was OK, was Mary. Loved her bird watching. That was her passion. That and *Heaven's Harvest*.'

'The TV soap? I never quite got into it, but it's fun seeing Didlinton locations. That's the only reason I sometimes watch it.

'So, you and Mary were friends. Did she tell you why she went to the cliff path that day? She was meant to be travelling to visit her sister.'

'Was she? How did you know that? Oh, wait a bit, you've met young Simon. You should ask him out.' There was a twinkle in Harry's eye.

'Harry!' Poppy gasped, 'I'll do no such thing. Simon and I are simply friends.'

'We'll see how that turns out.' Harry

grinned. 'Anyway, we were talking about Mary, weren't we. No, she didn't tell me why she was on that path although she'd told me she was going to visit her sister. I saw her that morning, I told the police that. Saw someone else too — but they weren't interested. They think an old man like me is dithery.'

'Who else did you see?' Poppy asked, not wanting to be nosey but unable to help herself.

'I saw another woman, dressed like a jogger. These days they all wear that yellow Lycra stuff. Blinds the eyes, it's so bright.

'I was out digging for worms for my fishing along a stretch of beach. I'd seen Mary leave her cottage and pass by my living room window earlier. I didn't see her on the cliff path but then, my eyesight isn't as good as it used to be. But I did see someone wearing a lurid yellow top up there. Might mean nothing. In fact, it probably does mean nothing. I don't know what time I was there. I told the police that. I don't wear a watch these days.'

Poppy hid her disappointment. Any number of people could have used the path during that day. Unless Harry knew the exact time, he most probably saw a jogger who had nothing to do with any of this.

'Thanks for the tea, I'd better get back and feed the cats. Delilah isn't at her best.'

'I'll bring her some fresh fish if I catch any today. That'll perk her up.'

Poppy left Harry listening to his radio and went out of his gate, intending to go into her own cottage and search for cats. She hesitated and on impulse crossed the narrow street and went to stand under the street light. This was exactly the spot where she had seen the shadowy figure the night before.

She glanced down at her feet. There were no cigarette stubs or footprints or any other clues. Not like there always were in the black and white films from the 1930s. The detective always managed to find a clue under these circumstances.

Smiling at her own whimsy, she glanced up — and froze.

In this exact position, she was staring just as the figure had stared. Not directly at Gilly's cottage as she had imagined. Instead, the line of sight was Mary Soull's cottage.

Poppy checked again to be certain. She focused on remembering where she had seen the person. How they had angled against the street light. Yes — she was sure. Someone was watching where Simon now lived.

She wanted to run and tell him, but common sense prevailed. She would tell him, but it wasn't an emergency. It wasn't as if the figure was still there. Simon might think it was an excuse for her to visit him. She didn't know him well enough to go bursting in with a strange story.

So she went home first. There was a strange odour in the cottage.

Going upstairs, she noticed the door to the tiny airing cupboard was ajar. She was about to shut it when she heard a noise. Peeping inside, with a frown, she saw Delilah reclining on one of Gilly's best bath towels. And she wasn't alone.

4

'Four, is it? Oh, wait, there's five. Poor little chap, he's half under his siblings.'

'He doesn't seem to mind, though. He's suckling just as much as his brothers and sisters. How lovely — two black kittens, two white and a black and white one. I must write to Aunt Gilly today and tell her. I hope she'll be pleased — I know she believed Delilah was neutered.'

'Write to her? Can't you just text her?'

Poppy and Simon were standing outside the airing cupboard, looking inside at a very smug Delilah and five tiny, warm and squirming kittens. Poppy hadn't thought twice about running next door to share her excitement with Simon.

His reaction had been a wide grin that lit up his blue eyes. He'd put down a sheaf of papers he was holding and gone with her to view the new family.

'She doesn't use her mobile on holiday. Says she wants a complete break from her day-to-day life and doesn't want to see the news or Facebook or her cousin's moany texts.'

'But what if something happens and someone needs to contact her?'

'If it was an emergency, then the police could contact her, she told me. I do have her address in France. Anyway, I sort of like writing letters. Especially letters that have good news. I'll get a card with a cat on it. She'll like that.'

'Shouldn't we clean up in there?' Simon nodded towards the cupboard. 'It's a bit . . . musty.'

'I know what you mean, but I think we should leave Delilah to get used to her new babies first. I'll try to move her later and get some clean cloths for her to lie on.'

They stood on the landing. Poppy felt suddenly awkward.

'Look, I'm sorry I disturbed you. You were obviously hard at work sorting out your cottage.'

'I'd much rather be here seeing this,' Simon said, and he sounded sincere.

Poppy felt relieved. She didn't want him to think she was making excuses to see him. It was strange how her first impulse had been to share her joy with him.

'Do you fancy a quick sandwich? I was going to make a late lunch for myself. I was round visiting Harry and stayed longer than I realised. You don't have to. In fact, you probably don't want to, I've delayed you enough. You're so busy.'

'Now I'm not sure if you want me to stay or if you'd rather I left,' Simon said, quirking an eyebrow.

Poppy laughed and felt her tension ease away.

'I'd like it if you stayed.'

'That depends on what's in the sandwich,' he teased.

'Ham and salad any good? I went to the shops this morning for the ham, and I've still got vast heaps of lettuce leaves from Harry's offering left.'

'Sounds great. I'd be glad of a break from all the paperwork, to be honest.'

'That bad, eh?'

Poppy led the way downstairs to the kitchen and began to make two door-stopper sandwiches and a pot of tea. Once the food was on the table, they sat companionably.

'It's difficult going through Mary's personal items. It's someone's life. Also, my mother called me. She's still convinced Mary was murdered and wants me to find out more about the circumstances.'

'And will you?' Poppy finished her sandwich and pushed away her plate.

'I don't know. Seems like a wild goose chase to me.'

Poppy knew she had to tell him. Her fingers circled her hot mug of tea nervously.

'I don't know if this has any bearing on it or not,' she began, 'But, last night, there was someone watching your cottage.'

Simon's eyebrows rose and he put his sandwich down.

'I know, I know, it sounds crazy,' Poppy said hastily. 'I keep asking myself if I imagined the whole thing.'

'No . . . no, it's just . . . not what I was expecting to hear,' he said, shaking his head. 'Who'd want to watch the cottage?'

'I've no idea. It's weird. But what if it's connected to Mary's accident in some way?'

'How? Could it just have been a passer-by stopping to tie a shoelace or smoke a cigarette?'

Poppy took a breath in and considered that. Was it possible she was making a mountain out of the proverbial molehill? Was there an innocent explanation?

'Whoever it was wasn't smoking. I think I'd have seen the smoke or a dropped fag end. And I didn't see them bending down to their shoes. In fact, I think that's what made me think it was suspicious. The fact that the figure was so still. Just . . . staring.' She shivered.

Simon shifted in his chair. His brows knitted in thought. Then he looked across at Poppy.

'Maybe Mum's right. There is something to investigate. And even if I find out there is nothing suspicious, it'll put her mind at rest.'

'So . . . you mean you're going to snoop around?'

Simon's smile was strained. 'I think so. After all, I've got all summer. I was going to mess around on the water, hire a boat, read that pile of books on my Kindle, but I can do some Sherlocking too.'

'Sherlocking? Is that even a word?' Poppy paused. 'Would you like a Doctor Watson to help you?'

The words came out of her mouth before she could stop them. She hadn't thought it through. But she knew she wanted to help him. Besides, with her curious nature, she couldn't help it. She needed to know what had happened to Simon's aunt.

'Really? You'd help me?' He seemed ridiculously pleased and Poppy felt a warm glow in her chest at his relieved expression.

She nodded.

'I'd love to. I've got loads of free time too for the next few weeks. So, how do we begin?'

* * *

There was a fresh breeze as they walked along the roadside pavement that led out of the village. It cut through Poppy's cotton T-shirt and she felt the goose-bumps rise on her arms. The wind whipped her hair into her face and she tucked some curls behind her ears. She glanced at Simon but he looked lost in thought. His dark hair had turned spiky in the rushing air and his cheeks were flushed. His hands were tucked into his pockets and his shoulders hunched forward.

They had quickly finished their lunch and Poppy left the dishes in the sink to wash up later. She fed Bubbles and Geoffrey, making sure their bowls were wide apart in case of spats, and took a dish and some water up for Delilah.

They had decided that the first action was to check out the scene of the accident. Going to the cliff path where Mary had fallen would at least give them an idea of the surroundings.

The sky was turning grey now and

64

the temperature had dropped. Poppy wished she'd brought a jacket. The road out of the village curved to the left, and she knew it then continued on for a few miles between fields until it reached the next town. On the bend of the curve, the pavement turned to dirt track and forked to the right. There was a stile over a wire fence, and the track then wound up a gentle slope to the headlands and the cliff path.

She followed Simon's tall figure over the stile and into a large field of intensely green grass. In the distance there were sheep peacefully cropping. Below their feet the grass was springy and dry. There was a scent of summer, crushed herbs and fresh air, with a faint smell of coconut from the gorse bushes scattered along the field edges. To their right, where the sea was visible, they heard the shriek of seagulls and the far off sound of a ship's horn.

'It's rather blowy,' she observed, catching up with Simon's long stride.

'Yes, we'll need to be careful on the

cliff path. At least it's not raining. Then it can be treacherous.'

'I wonder what the weather was like, the day Mary fell.'

'Actually,' Simon said, glancing over at her, 'I checked that. It was a dry day with middling temperatures. The path would have been OK.'

There was a thudding behind them and then a jogger passed with a quick 'hello'. Ahead of them, there was a person walking with two Labradors.

'It's less busy than I thought it'd be up here,' Poppy said.

'The weather isn't that nice, so I guess that's probably why.'

'Harry told me no one admitted to seeing the accident,' Poppy said, thinking out loud. 'A dog walker on the beach found her. He did tell me that he saw a female jogger in yellow Lycra on the cliff path. If it was a nice day, I wonder why it wasn't mobbed?'

'Yeah, it's strange. We're nearly at the split in the path. Can you see it?'

Simon was puffing slightly as the

incline sharpened. Poppy's heart was thudding and she breathed hard, unaccustomed to the exercise.

I really must start jogging again, she thought.

She squinted towards where Simon was pointing. The path they were following kept winding up the steepening grassy slope, parallel to the white, chalky cliffs. But a smaller path diverted under the bluffs and disappeared behind the tufts of rushes and rock rose.

'This is roughly where it happened,' Simon said, indicating the lower path. 'Shall we?'

Poppy nodded, feeling apprehensive but not wanting to look afraid. She let Simon go first. Concentrating on placing her feet carefully helped her focus.

The lower path was cut into a ledge in the cliff face. It was wide enough for only one person. The path surface was crumbly white pebbles, and she felt her trainers slip and then grip.

'This would be awful in bad weather,' she called to Simon.

The breeze whisked her words away. She leaned in, putting a hand on the bank. There was a good metre of width of grass between the path and the edge. That meant that she was safe — it just didn't feel that way.

Simon looked back. She must have looked scared because he stopped.

'OK?'

She nodded. 'It's a bit . . . airy.'

'I know. Do you want a hand?'

He put out his hand and she gripped it gratefully. His hand was warm. A tingle shot up her arm. Nothing to do with being on a cliff path with a terrifying drop to the beach below. All to do with his touch. Poppy felt her colour rise. She hoped it wasn't obvious.

Simon went along the path slowly, leading her forward. Then he stopped.

'Look, there's a bench here.'

There was a natural alcove set into the rock and a wooden bench had been installed there. Poppy sat down. It felt secure. Simon sat beside her and for a moment they simply stared out at the stunning view. In front of them was the sea that stretched to the horizon. The path edge was fringed with yellow rock rose and pink sea thrift bobbing in the breeze. Gulls rose up as if from the earth, calling to each other. Below them, between two headlands of jumbled rocks, was a narrow stretch of yellow sands.

Seabirds of different kinds perched on the sides of the headlands. Out on the sea itself, more floated on the surface and overhead plenty were flying about.

'A perfect place for birdwatching,' Simon remarked.

'Do you think this is where she sat with her binoculars?' Poppy said.

'Yes. It must be. There's nowhere else that I can see.'

'Which means she had an amazing view of that beach. It's kind of secluded, don't you think? I don't imagine many people use it. It's so far from the main beach and quite hidden by the rocks.'

'You're right. What if . . .' Simon stared at the beach and then at Poppy. 'What if she saw something, or someone on that secret beach?'

'And what if she then confronted them with that information . . .' Poppy trailed away, her imagination taking over.

They sat on the wooden bench, in the buffeting wind, and stared down at the empty sands.

★ ★ ★

'As it happens, Mary's best friend is called Mina — not Moira or Manda,' Simon said.

They were sitting in his car, on the side of the street where Mina Hendry lived. She was on the other side of the village and it was hardly a long walk from Mary's cottage, but the car was a good hideout and a method of a quick getaway if needed.

'How did you work that out?' Poppy asked, nibbling a fingernail.

'There were a couple of postcards that she'd sent to Mary from her holidays. They didn't have her address, of course, but it was easy to find out. Mina is an unusual name and Harry gave me directions here.'

The houses along the street were pebble-dashed, identical semi-detached family homes. There were no old-fashioned cottages here. It looked like an estate that had weathered well over the years, with established mature trees and neat driveways. A group of children were playing with bikes and a football at the far end where the street ended in a cul-de-sac.

Mina Hendry's house was in the middle of a long row, with no particular features to make it stand out from its neighbours. There was a black painted gate with a small, neat privet hedge either side of the path up to the front door. The house looked well maintained from the outside.

'What are we going to say to her?' she said. 'Is this crazy, just turning up on her doorstep at eight in the evening for a chat?'

Simon shrugged. 'It was better to wait until after dinner. We'll be honest and say we're trying to find out Mary's state of mind before she died.'

'What do we know about Mina already?'

'We know that she was Mary's best friend, according to my mother. Harry seemed to back that up, or at least he didn't say that she wasn't. In fact, I also know that she's the same age as Mary because Harry said he overheard them talking about their big six-o coming up and they were only a month apart. That was earlier this year.'

They looked at each other. Poppy nodded.

'OK, let's do this.'

They rang the door bell three times before it was answered. Mina Hendry looked older than her sixty years. Her hair was white and her skin lined in grooves from her nose to her mouth. She was taller than Poppy and what Gilly might have referred to as big-boned. She frowned at them.

'Yes?'

Behind her in the dimly lit hall, Poppy

saw a man briefly before he disappeared from view.

'Hello, Mrs Hendry, I'm Simon Carruthers. Mary's nephew. This is my friend Poppy Johnson. We were wondering if we could come in and talk to you about Mary.'

'Mary's nephew. Goodness me. It was a terrible thing, the accident. But I'm not sure I've anything to tell you about it.'

There was a trace of an Irish accent in her voice. Her expression was difficult to read. Surprise, certainly, Poppy thought — but something else fleetingly passed over her features too before she simply looked sad.

'Could you spare us ten minutes anyway?'

Poppy smiled prettily. 'You might remember something or be able to share some memories of Mary.'

'Of course, of course. Come away in. I'm forgetting my manners, so I am.'

She opened the front door more widely and turned back into the hall, inviting them to follow her. The house smelled of beef and cabbage and as they passed an open doorway, Poppy saw the remains of dinner, empty scraped plates and a casserole pot, on a dining room table. Somewhere, there was a bowl of over-ripe fruit.

The house was very neat, tidy and traditional with magnolia-coloured walls, framed prints of countryside scenes adorning them, and old wood furniture. The kitchen, where Mina led them, was in country classic style. There was a solid oak table and matching set of chairs. A Welsh dresser sat along one wall with a selection of blue and white Delft china. The sink gleamed spotlessly and beside an equally shiny aluminium kettle there was a teapot covered in a crocheted tea cosy. A tray was laid with two teacups and two plates, and a selection of biscuits was spread out in a china dish.

'We're sorry to disturb you at your dinner,' Poppy said. 'Should we come back another time?'

Mina hesitated but then shook her

head. 'It's fine, I'm finished with dinner. Can I offer you both a cup of tea?'

Simon smiled politely. 'If it isn't too much bother, that'd be lovely. Thanks.'

Poppy and Simon sat at the kitchen table while Mina bustled about making tea, warming the pot and adding a third cup to the tray. She brought it over to the table and offered them biscuits.

'I was about to have a cup anyway when you rang the bell,' she smiled. 'It's nice to have company.'

Poppy wondered about the man she'd seen. But there was no mention of him. Mina poured the tea and glanced at them both.

'So, what did you want to know about Mary?'

'You were best friends,' Simon said.

'Well, we were friends at any rate. I'm sure Mary had other pals, I'm sure I do too. I lived in London all my working life, having come over from County Clare at eighteen to take up a secretarial job with the post office. I didn't move here until I took early retirement four years ago.

And that's when I met Mary, through the community group that keeps the village looking nice.'

'Can you tell us anything about her state of mind shortly before the accident?' Poppy asked.

'She was no different than usual. She was looking forward to the summer festival we hold in the village. But who knows what's in someone's personal thoughts? I'm sorry, I can't add anything to that.'

'Perhaps it wasn't an accident,' Simon said suddenly. 'She could have been murdered.'

There was a crash as the plate of biscuits slipped from Mina's hand and broke on the tiled floor. For a few minutes, the three of them gathered crumbs and shattered ceramic shards while Mina muttered apologies over her clumsiness. When it was cleared away, they sat back at the table.

'Who's saying it was murder?' Mina asked, her face grey with shock, and the lines around the sides of her mouth more pronounced.

'Not the police,' Simon said, 'But my mother believes there's more to it than meets the eye.'

'There is something I could tell you about Mary,' Mina said, pulling herself upright in her chair. 'She was very interested in that *Heaven's Harvest* TV programme. You know, the one that films right here in Didlinton. Particularly in the lead character, Hector. Well, he's not Hector in real life as you know. He's played by Brandon Tulloe.'

'She was interested in Brandon Tulloe?' Poppy asked.

Mina nodded. 'Yes, indeed. Like teenagers are star-struck with their pop idols. Mary was half in love with him. Very interested . . . some might say obsessed.'

* * *

When they said their goodbyes and got back in the car, they sat for a moment.

'What do you think?' Simon said eventually.

77

'I think she's mourning for Mary. She was very sad.'

'But? I am hearing a 'but', aren't I?' Poppy shifted in the passenger seat.

'I don't know. I saw the dinner table set for two people. There were two cups laid out for tea. But she never mentioned her husband at all. Even though I'm sure I saw him in the hallway when we arrived.'

Simon frowned. 'Maybe she's an independent sort. We didn't ask about Mr Hendry, so she didn't see the need to mention him.'

'Then there's the idea that apparently Mary was infatuated with Brandon Tulloe. What do we make of that?'

'I don't know if that's odd. Plenty of people have favourite actors.'

'I suppose so.' Poppy yawned. 'Let's go. I'm shattered, I need my bed.'

She didn't go straight to bed when she got back to her cottage. She locked up, checking each lock twice. She checked on Delilah and the kittens who were all asleep in the linen cupboard, and refilled her food and water dishes. Bubbles was absent but Geoffrey made an effort to come and greet her, his plumy tail waving high in welcome.

'Do you like the card?' she asked him.

She had picked up a card with a picture of a kitten on it, in a shop on the way back from the cliff walk. Now, she picked up a pen to write a note to Gilly about Delilah and the new additions to the family.

But her pen hovered over the card. Should she mention what she and Simon were up to? In the end, she decided not to worry Gilly.

As she signed off with love and a flourish of her signature, a little feathery tickle stroked the back of her brain. There was something she had to ask Gilly. But for the life of her, she couldn't remember what it was.

5

The main street in the village was closed off at both ends. There were TV vans and lots of equipment, along with people in black T-shirts with furry microphones, clipboards and cameras. *Heaven's Harvest* was being shot on location.

Poppy squeezed in amongst the other onlookers. They were being kept at a reasonable distance from the cameras and action but she could see that the action was set against a backdrop of the quaint village shops. There was a group of bored-looking extras sitting in plastic garden chairs while a woman scribbled something onto a sheet of paper. Maybe she was signing them in for the day, Poppy thought.

'Oooh, there he is,' a middle-aged woman next to her in the crowd squealed.

'Oh, isn't he lovely,' her companion sighed.

Poppy followed their adoring gazes to

see a tall, broad-shouldered man stride out in front of the village coffee shop and swing round with a charming smile for the cameras.

'Excuse me,' she said politely to the two women. 'Who is that?'

They looked aghast that she didn't know.

'That's Brandon Tulloe. He's the hero for this series.'

'What happened to John Bark?' Poppy asked. On her previous visits to Didlinton, she had seen some of the filming with the heart-throb. The two main characters had been John Bark and Lucy Sweeting, played by two well known soap actors.

'John swept Lucy off her feet and they went to live in Hawaii. Now Hector Rockford has bought the mansion and lives there with his ailing wife.'

'Thanks,' Poppy said, hiding a smile. The way the woman spoke, it was as if Hector, John and Lucy were real people. Still, that was the joy of soaps. They were intriguing and felt authentic if done well.

Especially if filmed against a local setting.

She stared at Brandon Tulloe. He was very handsome, and she could quite see how women would be drawn to him. He was too old for her, of course, but he had a rugged stance and solid build that suggested cowboys on the range and muscle for hire.

She wriggled her way through the crowd, with apologies, trying to get closer to see him properly. Eventually, she had moved a semi-circle to the other side where she had a much better view.

From there she saw that he was actually a great deal older than at first glance. His black, slicked-back hair owed much more to a bottle rather than nature, she guessed. And those piercing blue eyes? She'd bet they were contact lenses. However, he did have a certain presence, she had to admit.

He was wearing a pair of tight blue jeans which emphasised his thighs, and a sheepskin jacket with the collar turned up high. A pair of sunglasses hung casually from the front pocket of the jacket. As Poppy watched, a young woman ran in and adjusted the glasses. She had a large powder brush in her hand and she whisked this briskly over his forehead before leaving.

Brandon favoured her with a wink before the cameras rolled again and he caught his co-star in a manly grasp and swept his lips to hers. A thrilled murmur went round the crowd.

Meanwhile the extras were walking around, pretending to shop or drink coffee. It was all very entertaining, but Poppy needed a way to find out more about the star of the show.

She looked about for inspiration. Perhaps she could ask for his autograph in the break. But then what? She'd have two seconds to ask him . . . what? She found herself pushed back from the viewing by a group of women. Now she was close to the chairs where the extras had hung out. Sitting there was the young woman who had run over to fix the actor's make-up. She had a large set of boxes with bottles and jars and brushes and palettes. She was chatting to another woman about the same age. They were both dressed in strappy tops and cargo trousers.

'Are you up for a drink after this?'

'Absolutely. I'm desperate for a glass of prosecco right this minute. Still, only a thousand hours to go til the break. We're behind schedule on the location scenes.'

The make-up girl groaned.

Her friend patted her on the shoulder. 'Chill out, Tabby. You know the score. Brandon won't want to work any later than he has to.' She raised her eyebrows in a knowing way.

Tabby rolled her eyes. Poppy was intrigued. What were they referring to? She waited, hoping to hear more but Tabby stretched and stood up.

'Come along, Sam, better get back to the grindstone. I'll see you in the Fisherman's Arms later, yeah?'

There was no point in hanging about, as it was only early afternoon. Poppy headed back to the cottages and went to tell Simon what she'd learned. She hadn't seen him for a couple of days since their cliff walk. He had work to do, dusting and vacuuming the cottage, and she had done some of the tourist trail, visiting the nearby town and going to the museum and art gallery. After all, she couldn't spend the whole holiday being a detective.

'I'm going to head to the Fisherman's Arms for a drink and see if I can get talking to Tabby and her friend,' she announced.

'I'd offer to join you, but . . .' He indicated the mess with his widespread arms.

Poppy grimaced. The cottage was in complete disarray.

'Is it a case of omelettes and eggs?' she said. 'You can't make one without breaking the other.'

Simon nodded. 'Yes, there is method to my madness. I like to get vacuuming done properly. Also I lost my bank card but found it under the sofa.' He paused. 'Look, you don't have to do this, you know.'

'I know,' Poppy said. 'But I'm enjoying

myself. Sorry, that sounds dreadful. Your aunt has died, under tragic circumstances whatever turns out to be the truth, and I haven't forgotten that. But I quite like a mystery — and I need to know for certain what happened.'

Simon touched her arm and again she felt that involuntary tremor of attraction.

'Just be careful,' he said. 'Promise me?'

'Of course I will. Besides, it's just a drink with two girls. There's nothing to worry about.'

The memory of the figure in the darkness flicked into her mind but she pushed it away. She almost felt she had imagined the whole thing. She smiled up at Simon and he grinned back.

★ ★ ★

The Fisherman's Arms was busy even though it was a weekday evening. People had spilled out onto the pavement, chatting and drinking. Poppy had dressed carefully. She wanted to blend in and appear similar to Tabby and Sam so that they would be at ease with her. She'd chosen a strappy sundress, blue with tiny yellow flowers, and teamed it with wedge-heeled sandals. She had applied some light make-up, powder, blush and peach eye shadow, and a little glossy lipstick. Now, the problem was, how to get into conversation with them and make it seem casual and spontaneous.

She squeezed through the amiable crowd, unable to see the two young women outside. The interior was dark and cool and it took a moment for her eyes to adjust to the dim lighting. It was a traditional pub with brasses and dark, varnished wood. The carpet looked as if it dated back to the 1800s when the pub was opened.

The bartender was a woman with a pile of loose, bleached curls on top of her head. Her generous cleavage was on show thanks to a tight, pink blouse. Poppy wondered if she was an actress; it was such a cliché, just like a pub in a TV soap.

She stood at the bar, waiting to be served, and glanced around. Maybe she was too early. There was no sign of Tabby or Sam. She ordered a soda and lime, wanting to keep a clear head. Then, unsure of her next move, she walked further into the bar. She noticed people walking out at a rear entrance and followed a couple into a beer garden at the back of the pub.

There were wooden benches and tubs of roses and sweet peas. All the benches were taken and she saw Tabby and Sam at the far corner at a bench fringed by mock orange blossom.

Poppy hesitated. What was she to do? She could hardly walk up and ask to sit with them. As she stood there undecided, a man brushed past her unsteadily, jostling her and spilling her drink.

'Sorry,' he said, his eyes slightly unfocussed.

'Gordie!' Sam jumped up from the corner bench and came over to them. 'You're drunk, you idiot. Look what you've done.' She turned to Poppy. 'He apologises and he's going to buy you another drink, aren't you, Gordie?'

Gordie shuffled his feet, his face red with embarrassment. Poppy felt almost sorry for him but she was thrilled that she was talking to Sam and silently she thanked him for almost knocking her over.

'It's OK, it was an accident,' she said.

'Yeah, but you've only got half a drink there. Are you on your own? Want to join us? Least we can do is offer you a seat.'

'Thanks very much. It's a soda and lime,' she said, giving Gordie her glass with a smile.

Poppy could hardly believe her luck as Sam shepherded her towards the bench where Tabby was sitting. A few minutes later, Gordie returned from the bar and gave her a fresh drink. Tabby, Sam and Gordie seemed used to sitting with strangers and chatted easily with each other, giving Poppy time to catch her breath and sip her drink while she thought desperately how she could turn the conversation to *Heaven's Harvest* and in particular, its lead actor.

She needn't have worried. The

conversation was all about work. As she listened, she pieced together that Tabby was in make-up, Sam worked for wardrobe and Gordie was a general handyman on set.

'Are you a local?' Tabby asked her politely.

'No, I'm here on holiday.'

'We film the series *Heaven's Harvest* here. Me and Sam and Gordie all work on the set.'

'Wow, that must be so interesting!' Poppy gushed, eyes wide. 'I've watched that. Do you know Brandon Tulloe personally?'

'Yeah, I'm the girl who does his make-up.'

'What's he like?' Poppy tried to look like an eager fan.

Sam and Gordie were talking together, heads almost together, and she decided they were a couple. It gave her an opportunity to speak to Tabby on her own.

'He's very professional,' Tabby said. 'Great to work with. And he's very nice to everyone, not a diva like some people

I could tell you about. I've worked on quite a few TV programmes and some of the big names are just the worst. I mean it's hardly Hollywood, is it, so they shouldn't be so up themselves.'

Poppy was surprised that Brandon Tulloe was nice, and then felt that said more about her judging people than about him. Why shouldn't he be a nice person, just because he was rich and famous? She remembered Sam saying earlier that he wouldn't want to work late.

'It must be tiring though, working long hours filming,' she said with a sympathetic smile.

'Oh, it varies,' Tabby replied, taking a sip of her drink. 'Some days go on forever and we start at daybreak but Brandon likes to finish promptly which is great for me and Sam. Means we can get dinner at a decent hour and then a drink at the pub.'

'Why's he such a stickler for finishing on time?' Poppy asked, then wondered if she was pushing it too hard. Wouldn't

Tabby be suspicious of all her questions.

But Tabby was on to her third gin and tonic as she informed Poppy with a giggle and poked the slice of lemon around with her finger. She didn't seem to find Poppy's questions suspicious at all and Poppy put that down to the gin, the lovely evening glow of sunshine and the holiday mood of the people round about them.

Tabby waggled her eyebrows mysteriously and set her empty glass down on the bench table.

'Come on, I'll show you why Brandon doesn't like to work late.'

Poppy followed her out of the side gate of the beer garden. Sam and Gordie watched them with puzzled frowns but Tabby waved blithely and they went back to their chat. The pub was on the seafront and they looped round to the front of the building. Tabby led the way across the road to the promenade. She swerved left and began to walk along to the end of the village.

'Where are we going?' Poppy asked,

conscious that her sandals weren't made for lots of walking and generally gave her blisters after an evening out.

Tabby waved her arms genially in the air. 'Oh, not far.'

True to her word, shortly after that she came to a sudden halt. They were at the end of the promenade where a set of stone steps went down to the sandy beach. The rocky headland was near and the waves were splashing against it playfully. Gulls swirled above it, cackling. Further out, a yacht bobbed gently on the swell. Tabby leaned on the railings and pointed at the headland.

'See that?'

'The rocks, you mean?' Poppy said, trying to figure out what she meant.

Tabby nodded. 'Yeah, do you know what's behind them?'

Poppy thought for a moment. 'Yes, there's another small beach, isn't there? It's quite private. I've seen it from the cliff path.'

Tabby gave a small burp. 'Pardon me, that's the tonic catching me up.'

She threw Poppy a slightly unfocussed smile.

'The private beach?' Poppy prompted, desperately hoping to extract the information before Tabby fell over and slept on the pavement.

'Yeah, well that's where Brandon likes to take his lady friends for romantic picnics . . . if you know what I mean.'

'Oh,' Poppy said, eyebrows raised.

'Indeed.' Tabby nodded wisely.

'But it's not easy to get to. In fact you can't get there when the tide's high. He must have to be careful not to get stranded.'

'Don't be silly. He doesn't walk there over the sands. He's got *that*.'

Poppy followed Tabby's pointed finger and saw the yacht. It was white and chrome and sleek and screamed wealth. Of course it belonged to Brandon Tulloe. He didn't need to wait for the tides like ordinary folk. He could swim to and from his yacht — or perhaps he had a dinghy for his lovers to sit in to take them to the hidden beach.

★ ★ ★

'So, let's say Mary goes bird watching on the cliff path and she's sitting on the bench and sees Brandon in flagrante, as it were. That's a motive right there for him to bump her off,' Poppy said to Simon.

She had taken Tabby back to the pub and left her with Sam and Gordie who had bought another round of drinks in their absence. After thanking them for their company, she'd made straight for Simon's cottage to tell him what she'd learned. Simon looked pleased to see her and immediately made a pot of strong coffee, pushing aside the vacuum cleaner and a polishing rag he'd been using.

'She might have tried to blackmail him,' Simon mused. 'And then he pushed her off the cliff so she couldn't tell anyone.'

'Although it appears to be an open secret that Brandon takes his lovers to that beach,' Poppy mused. 'So, really, would it matter to him if Mary told anyone about that?'

'You said Tabby told you he has a jealous wife,' Simon reminded her. 'And one who holds the purse strings, by all accounts.'

'Well, Brandon obviously makes quite a bit of money himself from *Heaven's Harvest*,' Poppy said. 'But he hasn't been in anything else for a while so maybe his heyday is over. I did an online search on his wife and she's some kind of heiress to a fortune her dad's made with a chain of DIY stores. Perhaps if she found out Brandon was being unfaithful, she might kick him out and he'd lose his wealthy lifestyle.'

'It's a motive for getting rid of a blackmailer,' Simon said, pouring them both a second cup of coffee and pushing a plate of biscuits towards her. 'So, what do we do next?'

Poppy munched on a chocolate biscuit.

'We have to find out where Brandon Tulloe was on the morning that your aunt fell from the cliff.'

6

Simon sighed. It was a lovely evening and the sun was still high in the summer sky.

His mother had phoned earlier to ask about progress. They'd had another mixed communication, with Simon describing his day and the nice weather, and his mother asking about whether he'd discovered the murderer yet.

They had different notions of progress. She was disappointed he wasn't applying himself to the mystery full time, but pleased to hear he'd met Poppy and that she was helping.

He went out into the small garden, where a fluffy ginger cat was stretched out in the sun on the patio. The side gate creaked and he turned to see Poppy appear, smiling at him. Simon's heart took a double beat. She looked gorgeous. She was wearing a blue dress which complemented her shiny auburn hair perfectly, and a pair of high-heeled shoes which brought her emerald eyes almost in line with his. Her lips were a glossy red. It wasn't just how she looked, he thought. She seemed to glow from within with an everyday energy and happiness.

'Hi, are you and Bubbles having a chat? Can anyone join in?'

'Bubbles?' She'd thrown him with that. Or maybe it was the delicate scent of flowers she exuded as she reached him. He couldn't help breathing in a little deeper.

She nodded her head at the ginger cat. 'That's Bubbles. He looks innocent enough asleep but he's a bit of a menace when he's awake. Don't try to stroke him, is my advice.'

'OK, I'll remember that. Can I offer you a drink?' Simon said, remembering his good manners and trying to ignore how close she was standing to him.

'Thanks, but I'm going out. Tabby's invited me to a party that the *Heaven's Harvest* cast and crew are having. It's the perfect opportunity to try and find out Brandon Tulloe's whereabouts on the morning of the seventeenth of June. Do you want to come with me?'

'I can't,' Simon said quickly.

Poppy's face fell and he tried to think why he couldn't go with her.

'Too much to do here,' he mumbled. 'I'm filling in job applications for after the summer break.'

'Oh, right. That's fine, it doesn't take both of us to go. I was surprised to get an invite actually. I'd forgotten that Tabby, in her drunken state, had insisted on getting my mobile number for the party. I'll let you get on. Have a nice evening.'

She smiled and turned away towards the gate and the road.

'Wait!' he called. 'How about breakfast tomorrow at Katie's Diner? You can fill me in on what you discover.'

'Great — I'll see you then.' Poppy waved and disappeared.

He heard the creak of the gate as she went out, and felt a sudden disappointment that he wasn't going with her. A part of him wanted to run after her and beg her to wait while he got ready for the party.

The logical part of him warned against it. Yes, Poppy was stunningly attractive; yes, she was nice, and they seemed to get on well. But he had no intention of getting involved with anyone for a very long time. If ever. Suzie's betrayal had bitten very deeply. Simon doubted he'd trust any woman again.

So why had he arranged to see her for breakfast?

Only to find out about Brandon Tulloe so he could report back to his mother. That was it. Satisfied that he was thinking straight when it came to Poppy, Simon leaned down and stroked the cat's head. It opened its yellow eyes, shot to its feet, hissed and stalked away.

* * *

Poppy heard the party before she found the house. Tabby had given her directions. It was being held in a large property at

100

the top of the village. The house stood in its own grounds with borders of mature trees and leafy shrubs, far enough away from its neighbours to avoid complaints. Still, the blare of music and raucous laughter spilling from the open front door made her wince.

How was she going to hold a conversation with anyone in that atmosphere? And why was Simon so keen to avoid coming out with her?

The second thought popped into her head unannounced. It was hardly relevant to her task in hand. Sleuthing required total concentration, not visions of a dimple in someone's cheek or how deeply blue someone's eyes were when they looked at you.

He was probably right, though. The way he looked this evening, Poppy might have done something that would ruin their budding friendship. Like lean across, stand on tiptoe and plant a kiss on his lips. Or run her fingers through his thick brown hair. Or tease him until he grinned and that cute dimple appeared.

The thing was, none of that was good, she told herself. She hadn't been out with anyone since Alex, and for a good reason. He hadn't broken her heart, but he'd shaken her confidence in her ability to judge a man's personality and compatibility with her.

She didn't want to waste months in a new relationship only to discover that they had nothing in common and that he had been pretending to like cosy evenings in, Spanish wines and bluegrass. Alex, when he'd finally shown himself, preferred the city's night life, beer and loud, modern music with much beat and few melodies.

'Poppy!' Tabby shrieked and stumbled down the front door step. 'Come and get a drink. Sam and Gordie are inside.'

Poppy steadied her and Tabby hooked her arm and pulled her into a melée of heat, noise and a swirl of perfume, cigarette smoke and beer fumes. Poppy tried to look as if she was having fun as Tabby shoved a glass into her hand and began to dance to the music pulsating from a sound system in the enormous living room. Someone had pulled back an expensive-looking rug exposing a polished wooden floor as a makeshift dance floor and people were making good use of it.

The air was hazy with smoke. Through it, Poppy saw Sam and Gordie who waved at her before putting their heads together again to talk. Tabby was now dancing with a tall, thin guy in a navy shirt who had a glass of beer in both hands. Poppy wandered through into the hall, looking for Brandon Tulloe, and having to squeeze past people with many a 'sorry' and 'excuse me please'.

He was in the vast kitchen holding court, with an audience of mostly women watching him and laughing at his every word adoringly. He winked at Poppy as she came in. Some of the women glanced at her with hard eyes.

Really, she thought. *He's double my age. I'm not interested in him, so put the daggers away.*

More importantly, she wasn't going to

get anywhere near him to ask him any questions. Besides, what was she going to say? She couldn't very well just come out with it and ask him where he had been on the morning of the seventeenth of June.

She sipped her drink while she thought. The person she really needed to speak to was Brandon's personal assistant, she realised. Somehow she had to persuade them to let her see his diary for last month. She grimaced at the sweetness of the drink and put the glass down beside the sink. Tabby would know who Brandon's PA was. She fought her way back to the living room.

The writhing bodies on the dance floor had increased. She saw Sam and Gordie entwined in a slow dance that totally ignored the rhythm of the music. Where was Tabby? A man in a green jacket and too-tight trousers tried to speak to her but Poppy couldn't hear what he was saying. She smiled at him but that only brought his shiny face closer to her so she frowned instead until he moved away.

She had the beginnings of a thumping headache.

Tabby and her man in the navy shirt were in the middle of the dancing masses, she saw. There was no way she could reach her. Even if she did, Poppy doubted Tabby was in any state to answer a question sensibly. She made her way out of the room and into the garden, glad of the fresh air. She took a deep breath of it and went to stand under the trees for a moment.

She'd failed in her mission. Some detective she was. They were no closer to discovering if Brandon had killed Mary or not. It seemed ridiculous anyway now, standing under a large pine tree in some unknown person's lovely garden, watching partygoers laughing and chatting in front of the house.

She walked home, down the ancient, winding road that led from the top of the village towards the seafront. One street back was the row of familiar cottages. The lights were out in Simon's home. Poppy let herself in to Gilly's cottage and sighed with relief. It was quiet and peaceful, with no idiots spilling beer and leering at her. She went upstairs to check on Delilah and the kittens. They were still inhabiting the cupboard, but Poppy had cleaned it up and put in soft blankets. Delilah blinked at her sleepily and the kittens purred, a tiny ball of fur made up of five parts.

She went back downstairs and stared out the living room window, feeling suddenly lonely. Geoffrey roused himself from his snooze on the couch and came to greet her. The feeling of his fur on her bare legs was comforting.

* * *

Katie's Diner was a wooden hut on the beach, with an open counter facing the sea. There were several tables and chairs on the sand with parasols over them. Katie did breakfast, lunch and snacks most of the day but shut before dinner. The menu was short but delicious.

Poppy arrived at eight am and ordered

a coffee while she waited for Simon. She could have rung his doorbell but she hadn't seen any sign of life and they had agreed on a nine o'clock meeting. It felt good to sit and sip coffee and gaze out at the sea while a warm breeze teased at her curls. A few dog walkers went by, and all of them said good morning to her.

Simon arrived at a quarter to nine. They ordered bacon rolls and more coffee.

'How was the party?' Simon asked, squirting more tomato ketchup than strictly necessary onto his bacon.

'Useless,' Poppy said, taking a bite out of her roll and savouring the salty taste of bacon. 'I may as well not have gone. I learned zilch.'

'At least you tried. I'm sorry I didn't come with you. I . . .'

'It's OK, I know you were busy. Anyway, we'd only have both wasted an evening. It was more efficient, me going alone.'

They concentrated for a moment on eating, feeling slightly awkward.

'No sign of Brandon, then?' Simon said, breaking the silence.

'Oh, he was there. But I couldn't get near him for his fans and I couldn't get any sense out of Tabby who I predict will be spending most of today sleeping and drinking gallons of water.'

'Never mind. You tried. Want some ketchup?'

Poppy shook her head. 'Don't think you've left any in the bottle. How much ketchup does one bacon roll need?'

Simon laughed. 'It's a bad habit of mine. Ketchup with bacon, burgers, even steak.'

'Steak,' Poppy said, pretending to be shocked. 'How awful of you.'

They shared a laugh and the mood shifted so that both of them felt more relaxed with the other again.

'Why did you come to Didlinton for your holiday?' Simon asked.

'I come every summer,' Poppy said. 'Gilly lends me the cottage and I cat-sit for her. I love it. It's not for everyone, though. Too sleepy for some and not enough happening.'

'Someone in particular?'

Poppy smiled. 'My ex-boyfriend. Alex came with me last summer but he hated it. We'd been together for six months and I thought I knew him. It turned out that I didn't know him at all. He'd pretended to like what I liked but we were actually complete opposites. I wish he'd been honest with me from the start.'

'That must have been painful,' Simon said.

'I'm over him now. What about you? You said you were working in a boys' school but your contract had finished. It must be exciting to plan ahead.'

'I did say my contract had finished but that wasn't exactly true,' Simon said. 'The truth is that I left before my contract was up. I was engaged to be married to a girl called Suzie. I was very much in love with her and believed she felt the same about me. Instead, she cheated on me with one of my friends, Adam. They were both teachers in the same school so I had to leave. I couldn't bear to see them together.'

'Oh, Simon, that's awful.' Poppy instinctively reached for his hand and squeezed it gently. 'I can't imagine how you must have felt.'

He slowly took his hand from hers. Poppy blushed. She hadn't meant to touch him. It was only that she felt so sad for him.

'Coming here has been good for me,' he said. 'Even if I inherited the cottage under terrible circumstances, I am grateful to Mary for leaving it to me. It's been a distraction from losing Suzie and my job. Losing Adam, too — who was a good mate, or so I thought.'

'I can't think of anything worse,' Poppy said. 'My heart wasn't involved with Alex — more my pride in my ability to read people.'

'More coffee?' Simon stood up before she could answer and went to the counter to order.

Poppy stared at his broad shoulders and tapered back. He didn't want her pity, but she did feel so sorry for him. Simon was such a lovely bloke. He deserved better than a girl who broke his heart.

They walked back to the cottages after breakfast in easy conversation about the weather and the forthcoming summer festival in the village. Simon invited Poppy for another coffee and she agreed. She hadn't planned anything for the day except some reading, a bit of shopping for food and maybe a wander along the beach in the afternoon. How delightful it was to be on holiday.

She flicked idly through the pile of magazines in Simon's living room while he clattered about in the kitchen, shouting through to her about his books and how he was reading through magazines he'd found in the cottage.

Poppy cast a lazy eye over a garish gossip magazine and then sat bolt upright.

'Simon. Brandon Tulloe didn't kill Mary.'

Simon came through, balancing a tray of mugs. He frowned at her.

'You sound very certain. How do you know?'

She stabbed a finger at the middle spread of the magazine.

'Because he has the perfect alibi. Look. These are photos from a charity gala event of the celebs attending. See who is right there?'

Simon squinted at the page but Poppy shifted it back, excitedly.

'I'll read you the caption under the photo. *Sylvia Tulloe, heiress to the Brick & Paste fortune, and her actor husband Brandon attended the glittering event in London's West End on Sunday evening.* And, Simon, if you look at the information at the top, that's definitely Sunday the sixteenth of June.'

'He could have travelled up from London and still got here in time to throw Mary off the cliff on Monday morning,' Simon argued.

Poppy shook her head triumphantly. 'No, he couldn't. Because . . .' She flicked to the next page which was even more photos of celebs and food. 'On Monday morning, the celebrities visited local food banks and gave out food parcels to community groups and families. There's Brandon looking suitably humble with a tin of baked beans in his hand.'

'So, where does that leave us? Who else had a reason to murder Mary?'

7

Why had they considered Mary capable of blackmail in the first place? Simon thought, looking around at the living room which looked ordinary and rather nice. It was ridiculous to imagine his aunt blackmailing Brandon or anyone else. He and Poppy were being far too dramatic.

Although he did wonder how Mary had managed to buy all the new furniture. The paintwork in the cottage looked fresh, too. Her pension from her job as a secretary in a local office was modest and she didn't have much in the way of savings as he'd noticed from the paperwork. She must have had a nest egg somewhere and he just hadn't found it yet.

He could discuss it with Poppy. Perhaps she'd like another breakfast at Katie's Diner. Simon looked at his watch. It was eight am. Definitely a decent hour for toast and coffee or a nice bacon roll.

Then he stopped himself. He mustn't pester Poppy every time he needed a chat or to mull something over. It was just that she was so easy to talk to. He hadn't meant to tell her about leaving his job and about being jilted and cheated by his fiancée. But he had told her.

Funnily, he felt better after getting it out in the open. Although her sympathy had almost brought tears, and he'd had to get up and order more drinks to give himself a moment to blink them back.

He craved her company. There. He'd admitted it. It was hard to keep away from her. It was also increasingly hard not to act on his attraction for her.

Acting on that would be a disaster. He knew that. He wasn't ready for another relationship — perhaps he never would be after what Suzie had done. And Poppy wasn't the sort of girl he could casually date. She deserved better than that. She deserved more than he had to offer.

Simon sighed deeply. *Forget it.*

He went into the kitchen, cut some

bread and stuck two slices into the toaster. He boiled the kettle and put a spoonful of ground coffee into the cafetière. With a last brief longing for a bacon roll at Katie's, he spread butter and jam onto his toast and took his breakfast to the kitchen table.

Settling on a stool, he knocked his knee on a jutting handle. He bent down to look.

There was a drawer in the table that he hadn't registered before. Pulling it open, he found a notebook, like a school jotter. He flicked it open and grinned. Mary had written all her computer passwords in it. Which meant that finally he'd be able to access her laptop, which was upstairs in her spare bedroom. If there was any extra paperwork or correspondence, he hoped he'd find it soon.

* * *

'Oh, Delilah, you mustn't roll on Tiny,' Poppy said, trying to disentangle the warm bundle of purring kittens. 'He's not as strong as your other babies. You need to look after him a bit more carefully.'

Delilah didn't seem too bothered. She lay on her side with her eyes half closed while the kittens suckled. Well, four of them did, with little paws kneading their mother's belly. The fifth kitten was smaller than the others. His siblings kept pushing him out of the way or rolling onto him and he was too weak to get to the milk.

Poppy hadn't named the kittens, assuming that Gilly would give them away to good homes but she had named the runt Tiny. He had soft black and white patches but his fur was quite thin. She worried he wasn't thriving.

She was nearly at the back door on her way to discuss Tiny with Simon when she stopped. This wouldn't do. She couldn't go round to see him every time she wanted a chat or had a worry. They hardly knew each other. She might feel like she'd known him for ages but that might not be reciprocated. If only he wasn't so easy to talk to. It was hard not to go next door and share her concern about the kitten.

Instead, she went to visit Harry. It was mid morning and he came to the door rubbing his head with a towel.

'Hello, my love. How are you this fine summer morning? Come along in, I've got a lettuce for you, freshly picked, and a bowl of green beans. Nothing nicer than fresh beans from the garden, is there? Just let me get dried off.'

'Morning swim?' Poppy followed him in through the cottage and into the back garden.

Harry like to be outside when the weather permitted. He had a table and chairs on his back lawn. The ancient radio was in its usual place on the table with a local station playing oldies and goldies. The tarpaulin was stretched out in a corner of the garden. It looked as if it still needed some sewing.

'Yes, I've had my swim. Very invigorating it was too. It may be hot weather but the sea takes a while to warm up. Did my stretch along to the buoy and back. Sets me up for the day. I'll just be a minute.'

Poppy sat in the sunshine and put her face up to it, relaxing. She'd have put the kettle on but she knew Harry liked to do that himself.

Sure enough, he came out minutes later, hair dried, and bearing a tray of mugs and biscuits. He stifled a yawn as he sat down.

'Your swim's tired you out,' Poppy remarked, helping herself to a chocolate digestive. Harry had put a generous pile of them onto the plate. They were his favourite.

'No, love, it's not the swim. That's what wakes me up. I don't sleep much and I get up in the small hours and read. But sometimes I'm restless. I need a project other than reading a tome or two. Should be mending my tarp but it's cold outside at three in the morning.'

Poppy considered this.

'I might be able to help you with that.'

'With what?'

'A project. It's just a thought. Or, no,

119

maybe not . . . it's a bit much to ask,' she trailed off.

'Come on, my love. Spit it out. I'm not getting any younger waiting. If it's a good project I'll take it and give you two lettuces. If I don't like it, I'll soon tell you.'

'Well, you know that Delilah's had kittens?'

'How is she? Gilly's very fond of that cat. She'll be delighted it's sprogged.'

'That's the thing. Four of the kittens are doing well and Delilah is healthy and happy. But Tiny isn't thriving.'

'Tiny?'

'Yes, Tiny,' Poppy said, 'He's the runt of the litter and to be honest, Delilah doesn't appear to be taking care of him at all. He's hardly getting any milk and he's not growing as big as the others.'

'What does this have to do with my project?' Harry said. 'Although I'm beginning to get an inkling. Does it involve pipettes and night feeds?'

'Harry, you're a star.' Poppy leaped up and hugged the old man. 'I'll bring Tiny over later.'

'Wait a minute, I haven't said I'll do it yet,' Harry protested.

Poppy's heart sank.

'I thought you'd like it as a project. You're up in the night any way. But if it's too much for you, then I'll feed Tiny if I have to. I've bought a pipette and I've looked on the internet about how to feed little creatures with it.'

'I'm teasing you,' Harry grinned. 'Of course I'll take Tiny. And I'll pay you two lettuces for him. How's that?'

★ ★ ★

Poppy was thinking about weakling kittens and methods for sterilising pipettes when she went back to the cottage. She had a bag with two enormous lettuces double their weight with soil on their roots, and a bunch of French beans. She decided she'd get Harry a box of chocolate mints as a thank you and take them across that evening with Tiny.

Her mind was busy with these plans

as she squeezed past the dresser in the hallway, but her sixth sense apparently was working. She had a sense she wasn't alone even before she smelled the cigarette smoke.

Oddly, she wasn't afraid. She walked into the living room and stared.

A woman was lying on Gilly's couch. She had long red hair and wore an Indian cotton print dress that came to her ankles and leather Roman sandals. One arm was draped over the couch so that her fingers trailed to the floor while the other was held high with a home-rolled cigarette between her fingers. She blew a curl of grey smoke from between her lips. She had been staring at the ceiling but now she angled her head and her cat-green eyes fixed on Poppy.

'Hello, sweetie. Are you staying here too?'

'Angela! What are you doing here?' Poppy exclaimed.

'You could call me Mum.'

Not likely, Poppy thought. She waited for an answer. She wasn't going to show her mother how shocked she was to see her here. She had never turned up in the summer holidays before.

'Gilly gave me a key ages ago and said if I needed a place to stay, then to let myself in. So here I am.'

'I haven't seen you in three years and now here you are. Where have you been?'

Poppy tried and failed to keep a bitter tone from her voice.

Angela sat up and drew in from her cigarette.

'I was visiting friends in Goa and travelling around for a while. I only got back to England a few days ago and made my way here.'

'You can't stay here,' Poppy stated.

Angela stretched like a cat and stubbed her cigarette out on a dirty plate. She had obviously helped herself to a sandwich, going by the food remains on the plate. She swung her sandalled feet from the couch and planted them on the carpet.

'Take pity on me, sweetie. I've nowhere else to go.'

'You've got friends everywhere, or so you used to tell me. Why not go sofa surfing round all of them? I'm staying here for the summer, cat-sitting for Gilly.'

Angela waved her arm vaguely to encompass the small living room.

'Plenty of space for two, isn't there? I don't have much stuff, just my rucksack. I won't bother you, if that's what you want.'

Poppy sank down into one of the armchairs, feeling tired.

'Why now? Did something happen in India? Or have you run out of cash again?'

Angela threw her a reproachful look.

'That's hardly fair. I do work, you know. I write for travel magazines and I take local jobs as I move about. Your dad doesn't need to send me cheques.'

'Strangely, Dad still worries about you.'

'And what about you? Do you think about me?'

Poppy shook her head. 'Not really. Not for the last ten years certainly, since

I grew up and figured you out.'

'Ouch,' Angela pretended to wince. 'That hurts. I think about you a lot. In fact, I brought you a present.' She pulled a rucksack from behind the couch and rummaged in it.

Poppy felt slightly sick. She wanted to scream at her mother, sob and be hugged all at the same time. Angela always had that effect on her. She turned up like the proverbial bad penny, randomly, and just as Poppy was becoming fond of her, disappeared for another adventure leaving a scrappy note. It had been three years since she last saw her. Then, Angela had been in the Alps working in a ski resort as a cook. Before that, she was teaching surfing in Queensland off the Great Barrier Reef. And prior to that, Poppy couldn't remember the exact order of her locations.

Angela thrust a badly wrapped package at her. Poppy took it reluctantly.

'Go on, then. Open it up.'

Angela leaned forward, elbows on knees in anticipation. Her long red hair hung over her angular face.

A tiny part of Poppy was concerned that her mother wasn't eating enough. Most of Poppy decided it had nothing to do with her what her mother ate or didn't eat.

She opened up the paper wrapping. Inside was a painted wooden box with tiny brass hinges. It was pretty. She opened it. It was empty but exuded a faint scent of sandalwood.

'Do you like it? You can keep earrings in it, that sort of thing,' Angela said.

'Thanks.' Poppy hesitated, 'You can stay here if you want. There's a second bedroom.'

'Great.' Angela stretched and yawned. 'I might have a lie down, I've been travelling for days without a break.'

She lifted her rucksack and slung it on her back. She headed towards the door and the hall, where she turned back to Poppy.

'I'm back in England for good this time. I'm going to rent a place and settle down. You and I can get to know each other.'

Poppy didn't reply. She had heard this before from her mother and it had never worked out. Angela's feet were restless. Maybe this was why Poppy was averse to backpacking round Europe and preferred her summers in the same place every year. She needed the comforting routine that Angela had never provided.

'Have a good sleep,' she said. 'I'll call you when dinner's ready.'

★ ★ ★

Angela had barely disappeared up the narrow staircase and shut her bedroom door, when there was a loud knock at the front door.

Poppy opened it, expecting to see Harry. Instead, Mina Hendry stood there.

Poppy was struck once more by how tall she was. Her white hair was smoothed back and she had applied some face powder and lipstick. She was more smartly dressed too, in a dark green skirt and yellow blouse.

'Can I come in?' she asked.

'Of course. Sorry, you took me by surprise.' Poppy took her through to the living room, relieved that Angela was out of the way so she didn't need to explain either woman's presence to the other.

'What can I do for you?'

'Could I have a glass of water, please?' Mina asked.

Wrong-footed again, Polly went into the kitchen and poured two glasses of fizzy water and hastily put some biscuits on a plate for her unexpected guest. When she came back in, Mina had settled into an armchair and was staring around.

'It's my aunt's home,' Polly explained, 'She loves knick-knacks as you can see.'

Gilly's living room with its overflowing bookcases, ornaments, half-burned candles and variety of cushions and throws was quite a contrast to Mina Hendry's neat house.

Mina nodded but didn't comment. She didn't reach for the glass of water nor take a biscuit. She stared at her feet and then rubbed her hands together as if she was cold.

'How did you know where I lived?' Poppy asked.

'I saw the nephew's car outside his cottage but there was no answer when I knocked. I thought I'd ask here if they knew when he'd be back, but saw you through the window.'

'Was there something you wanted particularly?' Poppy asked, then realised she sounded a bit rude and uninviting.

'It's about Mary,' Mina said. 'You wanted to know about her. Your young man even mentioned the idea she had been murdered but surely you can't believe that? Have you discovered anything?'

Poppy didn't feel like sharing their investigation with anyone, so she shook her head.

'Nothing,' she said.

It wasn't a real lie. Brandon Tulloe was innocent so they hadn't discovered much there.

'I had an idea,' Mina said, shuffling her feet. 'Mary had an argument about a week or so before she had her accident. It's probably nothing but I remembered it after you and your young man left that evening. I thought you'd want to know.'

'Who did she argue with?'

'Liz Soames. I wasn't there but Mary told me about it. She was fuming with the woman. I can't say I ever liked Liz much either. Too full of herself by far. You know the kind. Can never admit when she's wrong, a know-it-all. She fair got up Mary's nose, whatever it was about.'

'And Mary didn't say what the argument was?'

'Not in so many words. She was that angry, she could hardly get the words out. I had the cold so I was wrapped up in myself and wasn't listening too much. Anyway, you might want to speak to Liz Soames, that's what I'm telling you. I don't have her number but she'll be in the book.'

Mina rose from the armchair and

Poppy took this as her cue to let her visitor out. Mina paused on the doorstep for a moment.

'You'll tell me if you find out anything.'

'Yes, of course,' Poppy said.

★ ★ ★

'She's sad,' Poppy said to Simon later that evening.

'Do you mean she's a sad sort or that she feels sad?' Simon asked, gesturing with a bottle of wine and two glasses.

Poppy smiled and he poured two full glasses, passing her one. 'Both, actually. It was kind of her to come and tell me about the argument. She didn't need to bother. She must be missing Mary. They were best friends. Friends are hard to replace as you get older.'

'True,' Simon agreed. 'We can try and track this Liz Soames down tomorrow, if you like. Or are you busy?'

'I'll be glad to have an excuse to get out of the cottage, to be honest.'

'Oh, why's that? Delilah and the kittens giving you bother?'

'Harry's got Tiny, so I'm less worried about the kittens now, and Delilah can cope with four. No, I need to get out because my mother has come to stay.'

'Your mother? You didn't mention that before.' Simon raised his eyebrows.

'That's because I had no idea she had a key to the cottage and that Gilly, her sister, had offered her to stay there.'

'And . . . you don't get on?' Simon asked.

'She's never been around long enough for me to know if we get on or not,' Poppy said wryly. 'Angela's not big on the whole maternal instinct. In fact, Delilah's a better mother to her offspring than Angela has ever been to me.'

Simon filled her glass again.

'I'm sorry about that. Mothers can be annoying but I feel they are kind of . . . essential . . . all the same. I love mine. Perhaps this is a chance for you and your mother to get to know each other properly?'

Poppy shuddered.

'Not happening. Now, have you got your phone so we can look up Liz Soames' number?'

8

Poppy glared at the mess in the kitchen. She had gone to bed at eleven, leaving Angela watching the large television and snacking on popcorn in the living room. She had been vaguely aware of her mother coming upstairs at around three am, hearing the creak of the old floorboards and the flush of the loo.

The kitchen sink was full of dirty dishes, a pan and several mugs, as if she'd used a clean mug for each drink. There were empty popcorn packets on the table, along with two empty soup cans. Around the toaster was a trail of crumbs and a smear of jam.

'I thought she looked underfed,' Poppy said to Geoffrey, who wound round her legs affectionately, 'But it looks as if she's had a second dinner to make up for it.'

The evening meal last night had been awkward with Poppy finding nothing much to say to her mother. Angela had described some of her long trip in India but spoke of people and places that Poppy knew nothing about and couldn't find common ground with.

She hadn't asked about Poppy's job or friends and Poppy hadn't volunteered any information. She had told Angela about her dad, and asked whether she would visit him. Angela hadn't confirmed this either way, which had upset Poppy anew.

She scraped cat food into Geoffrey's bowl and he ate greedily, plumed tail waving.

'And that's another thing. She's not smoking in the house,' Poppy said grimly, swiping a plate with stubs and ash piles off the table and depositing the contents into the bin. She put the dirty plate into the slimline dishwasher and filled the rest of it with Angela's leavings from the previous evening. She wiped the surfaces and sluiced out the sink.

'Hi — the door was open.' Simon's voice came from behind her.

'Hello! Come on in, the coast is clear,' Poppy grinned.

'Clear of what?'

'My mother.'

'Oh, I was hoping to meet her.' Simon sat on a kitchen stool, looking very at home.

'You'll have to wait for that pleasure as she's fast asleep and probably won't surface until late afternoon unless she's changed her habits.'

Simon's gaze flickered to the ceiling. Poppy shrugged.

'I found something,' Simon said. 'Something that might explain how Aunt Mary could afford new furniture and to get all her walls redecorated.'

'Do tell,' Poppy leaned forward eagerly. 'Was she blackmailing someone after all?'

'I don't think she was the type. Not that I knew her well, but it doesn't seem likely, does it?'

'I don't know. Probably, she slipped off that cliff path and it was an accident. We're only doing this to put your mum's mind at rest.'

'True.' Simon nodded. 'Anyway, I

found her laptop password and was able to get in and see her files. It turns out she was writing a book about bird watching. Not only that, she had a publisher and had been paid a very generous advance. There was email correspondence between Mary and her publisher and I found the final copy of her book in her folders. I also found an online bank account where the money was paid into.'

'She wrote a book! That's amazing.' Poppy got up and paced the kitchen, her finger on her chin, thinking. 'I think that might explain something Gilly said when she phoned me before I came down here. She said it was awful that Mary had died especially as she had just had some good news.'

'So, the good news was her book acceptance?'

'I think it must've been. Oh . . . and it might explain why Mary wanted to visit your mum.'

'She wanted to gloat about her book and her new wealth?' Simon said.

'Does that sound right?' Poppy asked.

Simon nodded. 'It would be in character for her, sadly. The last time she went to visit my parents unexpectedly was when she retired. She took the clock her work gave her and spent most of the visit talking about it and how much she was respected by her colleagues.'

Poppy made a face. 'That's sad. Sounds like she lacked confidence.'

'She must've been lonely,' Simon suggested.

'She didn't have to be, though. She had Gilly and Harry for neighbours. It could all have been quite different if she hadn't quarrelled with my aunt.'

'At least she had Mina. Are you ready to go and speak to Liz Soames?' Simon jumped off his stool energetically.

'You're enjoying this, aren't you?' Poppy laughed.

'It's giving a focus to my holiday. I hope I'm not enjoying it too much — and I really hope Mum is wrong and that it was simply a horrible accident.'

'Agreed,' Poppy said, slipping on her

light cardigan as it was a dull day. 'Where does Ms Soames live?'

★ ★ ★

Liz Soames lived in a detached house in its own grounds, five minutes drive north of the village. It reminded Poppy of the house where the dreadful party had been held, but this house was more moderate in size and the garden was considerably smaller.

They sat in Simon's car on the opposite side of the street.

'Did you phone her?' Poppy asked.

She stared at the property trying to decide what its owner would be like. It was an attractive house of golden sandstone with a mature creeper growing over the door. The garden was mostly lawn and a few tall trees grew near the boundary fence. The only garden colour was provided by scattered rhododendrons which had huge blossoms of crimson, pink and white. To the left of the blue front door, there was a bicycle leaning against the wall.

'I phoned her and said I was trying to meet Mary's friends and acquaintances to get a better sense of who she was.'

'What was her reaction?'

'There was silence for a minute then she said that I could come and see her. It was all quite civilised. She didn't mention any argument.'

'Let's go and see.' Poppy unclipped her seat belt and clambered out of the car.

They walked together up the gravel path to the front door. Poppy let Simon ring the bell. After all, Liz Soames wasn't expecting two visitors.

The woman who answered the door was slim with long, blonde hair and intelligent grey eyes. She was dressed in slim-fitting jeans and a loose pink shirt and her only jewellery was a gold bracelet on her right wrist.

'Simon Carruthers?' She had a cultured home counties accent.

'And this is my friend, Poppy Johnson.' Simon smiled. 'It's very kind of you to meet with us, Ms Soames.'

'Please call me Liz. Do come in. I apologise for the organised chaos. I'm going on holiday tomorrow for a fortnight.'

They stepped past the suitcase and bags in the hall as they followed her. Beyond the suitcase, another bicycle was propped up against the wall, the helmet slung over one handlebar and a small rucksack strapped over the back wheel.

'Sporty,' Poppy mouthed to Simon.

'So, how can I help you?' Liz asked, once they were all settled in her large, high-ceilinged living room. A large bay window with a window seat gave a view onto the lawn and the bright blossoms.

Liz had produced three glasses of home-made lemonade and apologised that she had no biscuits or cake to offer them. The room was neat and clean, with small, tasteful ornaments. A piano graced the far corner and there was a tall bookcase.

Sitting near it, Poppy was able to make out some of the book titles. There were several about health and eating well, self-improvement and travel and autobiographies of explorers and some of the classics — Dickens, Shakespeare and Jane Austen.

'As I said on the phone, I've inherited my Aunt Mary's cottage but I never knew her well and I'm trying to find out what she was like from her friends,' Simon said. 'I'd also like to know more about her accident if I can.'

'You're probably wasting your time with me, then,' Liz said with a slight smile. 'I wasn't a friend of Mary's.'

'How did you know her?' Poppy asked.

'Through the local bird watching club.' Liz took a sip of her lemonade, set the glass down carefully on its coaster and frowned. 'How did you get my name as a friend of Mary's, can I ask?'

'Mina Hendry mentioned you. To be honest,' Simon said hesitantly, 'she said you and Mary had an argument the week before she died.'

'Ahhh,' Liz raised groomed eyebrows. 'I see. Good old Mina. Never one to mind her own business.'

'Can you tell us what happened?' Poppy pressed. 'If you don't mind, that is.'

Liz got up and went to look out of the bay window for a minute before turning back to them. She ran her fingers through her hair, flicking it back behind her ears as if she was thinking. Then she nodded decisively.

'I've got nothing to hide. I knew Mary through the bird watching club, as I said. Occasionally Mina and her husband would attend if there was a special speaker so that's how I know her. Last year, Mary came to see me. She'd had an idea for a book about local bird watching areas and she'd managed to get a publisher interested in her proposal. She was very excited about it. She wanted me to contribute to it.'

Liz sighed and sat back down on the sofa, opposite Simon and Poppy. She looked suddenly tired.

'What sort of information were you to contribute?' Poppy asked, to get her talking again.

'You're not . . . *journalists*, are you? You do ask a lot of questions.'

'No, we just want to find out more about Mary and how she died,' Simon said earnestly. 'I'm her nephew, that's all. The police ruled it an accident and I'm sure it probably was.'

'Probably?' Liz threw him a look. 'So you feel there's a possibility it wasn't? That leaves suicide or murder. Which are you favouring?'

'Look,' Poppy said quickly, 'We're not accusing you of anything. We really do just want to fill in some details of her life. Please . . .'

Liz nodded. 'She wanted my research on robins for her book. I'm considered to be a local expert on *Erithacus rubecula* and I've carried out studies into their feeding behaviour and mortality rates in urban and rural locations. I was happy to give her my latest results and I drafted some pages of information for her book.'

'Is that your job?' Poppy asked, out of curiosity.

'No, no, it's my hobby, my passion. I'm a copywriter, I do marketing, that sort of thing for my money.'

'Why did you argue with Mary?' Simon said.

'When she showed me the final draft of her book and boasted about her advance I got angry. She'd taken my research and incorporated it into the book without any acknowledgement or mention of my name and she didn't offer me any payment despite the large royalties and advance payment she'd received. I challenged her and she basically told me it was her book, she'd written it not me, and I wasn't entitled to a penny.'

'Did anyone see you arguing?' Poppy said.

Liz chuckled but it wasn't a happy sound.

'I'd say about twenty people. I'd approached her at the end of one of the weekly club meetings. I never intended to get into an altercation but my temper rose and she was so obstinate and defensive that it got out of hand. You know, it wasn't about the money. I'm not rich but I live comfortably. For me, it was about her stealing my work and passing it off as her own. I simply wanted recognition that it was my research in that chapter of the book.'

Poppy remembered how Mina had described Liz Soames. Too full of herself and a know-it-all. But Liz didn't come across like that at all. She came across as someone who was quietly confident and knew her stuff. Poppy liked her.

'Sorry, could I use your bathroom?' she asked.

'Upstairs, top of the hall,' Liz said.

Poppy went through and up the stairs. She didn't really need to use the facilities but in any good crime story on the telly, the detective always asked to use the loo so that he or she could nose about the suspect's home. Poppy was too well-mannered to actually sneak into Liz's bedroom or the other rooms. She did go into the bathroom where she had permission to be, just in case there was a clue.

It was as neat and tidy as the rest of the house that she'd seen. There was a white sink, bath and toilet with tiled floor and a shower curtain with a pattern of flamingos on it. Nothing suspicious or out of place there. A dressing gown hung on a brass hook on the back of the door and a shower cap was hooked onto the heated towel rail next to two fluffy turquoise towels.

For good measure, she opened the bathroom cabinet and looked at its contents. Toothbrush, toothpaste, dental floss and mouth wash, shampoo and sun cream. Also athlete's foot powder and a tube of muscle heat relief. More evidence that Liz was the sporty type.

Poppy was about to go back downstairs when she noticed a white wicker basket between the side of the bath and the tiled bathroom wall. She paused. Was it a bit much to snoop in someone's dirty laundry? Still, who was going to know? She lifted the lid and peered in. On the top of the pile was a pair of black leggings, the shiny Lycra kind that runners wear . . . and a luminous yellow running vest.

What had Harry told her? He'd said he saw a jogger up on the cliff walk wearing a lurid yellow top. Could that have been Liz Soames?

If that was true, it placed her in exactly the same place as Mary Soull at the time of her death and she had a clear motive for murder. She'd been denied acknowledgement and a share of a considerable payment for her detailed research.

Her mind buzzing, Poppy went back downstairs where Liz and Simon had moved on from talking about Mary to chatting about gardening and birds.

They both looked up as she came in. Poppy wondered if her thoughts showed on her face.

'Liz, do you go running?' she asked.

Both Liz and Simon looked surprised at this change in topic.

'I run and cycle. Why do you ask?' Liz said.

'Were you out running along the cliff path on the morning that Mary died?'

Poppy said and felt as if her words bounced ominously off the walls and into the air around her. 'It was Monday, the seventeenth of June.'

Liz shook her head. 'No, I don't run there. The path's too chossy. I run along the beach, or out beyond here through the country lanes.'

'Chossy?' Simon queried.

'Too soft and unstable. I don't want to slip and break an ankle.'

She rose from the couch. 'Now, if you'll excuse me, I've got work to do today. I hope I've been able to help and I wish you all the best, Simon, in finding out more about your aunt. I'm sorry she came to such a terrible end.'

Poppy and Simon thanked her and went back to Simon's car. They sat for a few minutes after buckling up.

'What do you think? She seems really nice,' Simon said.

Poppy mentally rolled her eyes. Honestly, men saw nothing but a slim figure and long blonde hair. Although she had liked Liz Soames too. Until she found the running vest.

'She's lying about the running,' Poppy said. 'And we need to find out why.'

9

There was no opportunity to discuss Liz Soames further because when Poppy and Simon got back to Gilly's cottage, it was to find Angela and Harry enjoying lunch together.

The kitchen table had a spread of food; home-made bread, a tub of hummus, a plate of party sausages and a glass bowl of green salad. There was a tall bottle of elderflower pressé and two glasses laid out. They heard the sound of laughter before they saw them.

'Ah, there you are, you two. Had a nice walk together?' Harry winked knowingly.

Poppy blushed, even though they hadn't done anything wrong and most certainly had not been on a date, as Harry seemed to be implying.

'Want some lunch, sweetie?' Angela said lazily, waving at the food as if she owned the place. 'Hello, Simon, lovely to meet you. Harry's told me about you.'

'Lovely to meet you too,' Simon said warmly. 'Poppy told me you'd come to stay.'

He didn't have to sound quite so welcoming, Poppy thought crossly. Nor did Harry have to be enjoying himself in her company so thoroughly. She felt out of sorts. She almost wanted to turn on her heel and stomp out of the room, but that would be childish. How was Angela able to charm them so easily?

'I came to tell you how Tiny is doing,' Harry said. 'And I met your mother. Tiny, by the way, is thriving. He's put on weight.'

'That's great,' Poppy said. 'Thanks again for taking him on.'

'Harry's a real champ,' Angela said, as if she'd known him for ages, 'Up every four hours in the night to feed a kitten is dedication.'

'He's up in the night anyway or I wouldn't have suggested it,' Poppy said, defensively.

She wasn't going to have Angela take

the moral high ground. As if she possibly could!

'Salad and hummus?' Simon offered her. His smile was sympathetic as if he could read her thoughts.

The talk turned to more general matters for a while. Angela went upstairs to find some travel brochures she wanted to show to Harry. While she was gone, Harry snapped his fingers.

'That's what I meant to tell you. You'll recall I said I saw a runner in a yellow top on the cliff path the morning Mary fell? I know who it was now. It's been playing in my mind every so often. There was something familiar about her but I couldn't put my finger on it, so to speak.

'But it was Liz Soames, I'll bet my remaining teeth on that. She usually wears a pink or red top, not yellow. But her gait is peculiar, as if she leans to her left as she runs, if that makes sense.'

'That's a coincidence because we've just visited Liz to ask her about her relationship with Mary.'

Harry's eyes lit up with glee.

'Ah ha — so you are investigating Mary's demise. I suspected as much. What have you found out?'

'Not much but Liz lied and said she wasn't running that morning on the cliff path. Now, why would she lie unless she has something to hide?' Poppy said.

'Or Harry is mistaken and it wasn't Liz he saw,' Simon suggested.

'It was her all right.' Harry grinned. 'And I can take a good guess at why she lied, too.'

'Hold on a minute. You saw her quite a while before you saw Mary heading past your window in the direction of the cliff walk. Which means if she did push her, Liz had to wait about up there for ages. Is that likely?'

'If she was still angry, she might,' Simon said.

Harry stared at them both.

'Aren't you hearing me, you two? I know why Liz lied and I'm pretty sure she didn't kill Mary.'

Poppy and Simon stared back at him.

'Seriously?'

Harry chuckled. 'Liz has a boyfriend that she runs with. That's why I didn't immediately connect a single woman jogger in a yellow top with Liz who wears pink or red and has a running partner.'

'So where was the boyfriend that morning?'

'You'd have to ask him. His name's Derek Tallman and he works at the marine suppliers on the pier.'

'But why lie about being there?' Poppy asked, confused.

'Because Derek shouldn't be running with Liz. He's married to Carrie Tallman whose father owns the business.'

'I suppose that gives her a reason to lie if she did meet up with him for running. She wouldn't want us to know she had a married boyfriend. That makes sense to me. But the fact is, she was running alone that morning and that means she's still in the frame for killing Mary.'

Harry shook his head.

'I won't believe that. I've known Liz for years and she's a lovely woman. She's not a killer.'

'She was mad at Mary and there are about twenty people who saw them having a massive argument after the bird watching club meeting.'

'You can be angry at someone but not be violent. Heavens, if we were violent every time we were annoyed there'd be murders every hour or so. You want to go and talk to Derek, or go and speak to Liz again. I'm sure she has nothing to do with it.'

The clatter of Angela's feet coming down the stairs made them stop the conversation as if, by common agreement, they were not going to discuss it in front of her.

Or perhaps it was just too much effort, Poppy thought. Imagine trying to explain who the various suspects were and how they interlaced and why they even believed there was a murder in the first place.

'I found them eventually, at the bottom of my suitcase.' Angela waved a bunch of leaflets as she joined them. 'Did you visit the red fort at Agra, Harry?'

'I did indeed, in my youth.'

Harry patted the seat beside him and Angela spread out the leaflets, pointing out the information on the fort and other sights. Poppy and Simon joined in the conversation and the matter of Liz Soames, Derek Tallman and the mystery of Mary Soull's death were put aside for a couple of hours.

Later, when Harry was leaving, Poppy walked him over to his cottage so she could visit Tiny.

'You've got a wonderful mother,' Harry said.

'Really?'

'She's a very interesting lady. It takes guts for a single woman to travel the world. I have every admiration for her.'

Poppy hadn't thought of Angela like that. Her feelings for her were so mixed up she'd never considered her to be brave. She needed to consider Harry's words.

After seeing Tiny, she took her leave of Harry and went for a walk along the beach. Sometimes it was good to be alone with the breeze in your face and the salty smell of the sea and the seaweed. A dog was barking as it ran in and out of the waves, and its owner threw a frisbee to a small child along the stretch of golden sands.

It was hard separating the child Poppy's expectations of an absent mother and the adult Poppy's view of a woman she hardly knew. So far, she hadn't been impressed. Angela was untidy and too chilled out, as if she lacked direction. She might say she was back in England for good, but she'd promised this before and always let Poppy down. But Harry liked her and thought her brave.

The wind picked up and buffeted her and Poppy shivered. She went back home but ended up walking through Simon's gate instead of her own. She wanted company, but not that of her mother.

Simon had a bottle of ginger beer in his hand and a bottle opener. He smiled when he saw her.

'Excellent timing. I was about to have

a glass of this ginger beer to celebrate, but I prefer not to drink alone.'

'What are you celebrating?'

'It's a fresh start for me. I'm going to stay here and try to find a teaching post locally after the summer.'

'That's great. Are you sure you won't miss the city lights?' Poppy teased gently.

'I've never liked living in big cities. Village life will suit me perfectly.'

Poppy knew what he meant. She liked this way of life too. It was quiet, out of the way and peaceful. All the attributes that Alex had hated.

It was lovely to meet a man who felt the same way she did about the things that mattered. What a pity she had to return to Edinburgh at the end of the summer. She drifted into a brief daydream where she bought a cottage in Didlinton and worked in the same school as Simon and they got married and . . .

Poppy stopped herself right there. What was she doing? There was no sign from Simon that he was interested in her that way. They were friends — that was all.

'Calling Poppy back to planet Earth. Hello, hello, come in please.'

'Sorry, I was miles away. Are we going to go and find Derek Tallman?' Poppy said, accepting a glass of the fizzy ginger beer, to change the subject and get away from her own wild imagination.

'Let's do that. Although we should be prepared for the fact that he might not want to talk to us,' Simon warned.

'Good point. What exactly are we going to say? We're not the police or detectives or even journalists. So how can we explain our questions and general nosiness?'

Simon thought for a minute. 'We tell him what we told Liz. We're trying to discover what Mary was like, who her friends were and what happened to her. That's pretty much the truth anyway.'

* * *

The marine suppliers was one of a row of shops near the entrance to the pier.

160

The pier was the old-fashioned sort, with stalls selling ice-cream and sticks of rock and shellfish. At the end, there were small boats tethered and a set of metal steps going down to a pontoon. It cost fifteen pounds for a boat trip round the bay from the pier.

Next to the marine suppliers, there was an upmarket boutique, a sports outlet and a tourist shop selling buckets and spades and postcards. There was also an excellent fish and chip restaurant and takeaway.

Poppy pushed open the door and heard it chime. The interior was dark and cool after the glare of the afternoon sunshine. It smelt of diesel and rope and new tarpaulins. At the counter, serving an older couple, was a stout young man with buzz cut hair. Another man, taller and thinner, was hanging a stack of new raincoats onto racks.

'Which one's Derek?' Poppy whispered.

Simon nodded discreetly to the raincoat man.

'The other chap's too young for Liz.'

'He might be her toy boy,' Poppy joked.

'Excuse me, are you Derek Tallman?' Simon was already over at the racks and asking politely.

'Sure, how can I help you?' Derek had short sandy hair and friendly blue eyes.

He didn't look the sort to be cheating on his wife but you couldn't tell with people, Poppy thought.

'Can we ask you a few questions, please?' Simon said, awkwardly.

'What's this about?' Derek frowned.

Poppy stepped forward. 'If we can take a few minutes of your time, Mr Tallman, it would be appreciated. Is there somewhere quiet we can talk?'

Looking bemused, Derek Tallman led the way to a back room.

'Who are you?' he asked as they all went inside.

The room held boxes of stock, a shabby table, two scuffed chairs and a sink area with a kettle. Poppy and Simon stood and Derek didn't offer them a seat or put the kettle on.

'I'm Mary Soull's nephew,' Simon explained. 'I'm trying to find out more about her friends and what happened the day she died.'

'I'm sorry for your loss,' Derek said automatically, 'But I fail to see what this has to do with me.'

'We went to see Liz,' Poppy said. 'She was seen jogging up on the cliff path the morning that Mary fell off the cliff. A friend told us she usually runs with you. Did you see her that morning?'

'You don't seriously believe Liz had anything to do with Mrs Soull's death?' Derek said. 'That's ridiculous. It was an accident. I read about it in the papers. The police aren't looking for anyone in connection with it.'

'We're simply asking around,' Simon said. 'Liz was up there that morning. That's a fact. She and Mary had had an argument the week before. Maybe she was still angry, they had another argument and Mary slipped. I just want the truth.'

163

'This has nothing to do with me. I want you to leave now,' Derek said loudly. 'I don't have to answer your questions.' He gestured at the door.

Simon started to move but Poppy didn't budge.

'Does your wife know that you go running every morning with Liz?' she asked.

Derek seemed to deflate.

'Look, what do you want?'

'As Simon said, we just want to know what happened that morning. Why weren't you running with Liz as you usually do?'

Derek went over to the nearest scuffed chair and sat heavily. He rubbed his eyes with his knuckles and then glanced up at Poppy.

'I go for a run every morning before I start work. It keeps me fit and I like it. About a year ago I bumped in to Liz while she was running and we kept meeting each other and I got to know her. I'm not having an affair with her, whatever your friend told you. My wife wouldn't understand so I haven't told her, but it's not a secret that Liz and I run together. It's motivating to have a running buddy.'

Poppy nodded as if she understood.

'OK, I can see that. So, tell us where you were that morning.'

'I was late getting out. My son was teething and I was up in the night with him so I slept in. When I got to the cliff path, Liz was waiting for me. She'd run up and when I wasn't at our usual meeting place she'd done some stretching exercises and waited for me. I was only about ten minutes late. I arrived just after eight.' He shrugged. 'Then we ran as usual.

'There's no way she killed Mary. She didn't have time, and it's a crazy notion. Liz is a wonderful human being and totally gentle. She wouldn't hurt a fly.'

Poppy and Simon walked home from the pier slowly, eating ice-creams which dripped from the cones down their wrists.

Poppy licked the sweet liquid from her skin and bit the end of her cone off. Crunching on it, she said, 'So, do we think Liz did it?'

Simon was eating his ice-cream at a more leisurely rate than Poppy. She noted enviously that he still had most of a scoop on his and of course, the full cone itself. The ice-cream wasn't melting as messily, either. Some people were like that.

'No, Liz is off the hook,' Simon said. 'The police told Mum that Mary fell at around eleven. A dog walker found her shortly afterwards. We should have asked Liz what time she goes running. Then we wouldn't have had to speak to Derek. They were up there far too early to be suspects. Liz must be very fond of Derek to lie for him.'

'Good to have confirmation of the timings, though,' Poppy mumbled through the last flaky pieces of the cone.

'Here,' Simon grinned at her and gave her his paper napkin.

'We're at another dead end,' Poppy said. 'First, Brandon Tulloe turns out to be squeaky clean and now Liz Soames. She isn't even having an affair like Harry said, if Derek is telling the truth. Harry's such a terrible gossip, he loves to exaggerate.

'Are we just wasting our summer? Shouldn't we be eating ice-creams and hiring a boat and sunbathing on the sand?'

'Mum keeps phoning for updates,' Simon agreed. 'I should tell her it's over. There's no mystery to be solved. We've run out of suspects in any case. Who else had a reason to top her?'

'Do you fancy going out for a meal this evening?' Poppy asked, 'We can eat and talk about normal things and forget about Mary. I noticed a new fish restaurant on the seafront with good reviews.'

They were back at the front gate of Simon's cottage now.

'Sounds fun, I love fish — ' Simon was saying. He pushed on the gate and it swung open. 'That's odd, I'm sure I latched it.'

'The wind probably shook it,' Poppy said vaguely, thinking ahead to what she might order at the restaurant. She was a great fan of scampi and chips but perhaps she should be more adventurous and try an exotic dish like red snapper or octopus.

'Someone's been in here,' Simon said, staring around at his living room. 'That chair's been moved slightly and that drawer wasn't open when I left.' He went over to the cabinet where he stored his paperwork and began to open drawers and check the contents.

'Are you sure?' Poppy demanded. 'Has anything been taken?'

Simon looked about. He ran upstairs and came back down. He shook his head.

'My laptop and iPad are untouched and I had about a hundred quid beside my bed and it's there. Whoever was here wasn't looking for valuables. So, what were they looking for?'

* * *

They discussed it later, walking down to the sea front for a meal. Poppy wore a blue dress, cream cardigan and shoes with low heels in case they went for a walk after dinner. Simon had put on a tie, polished his shoes and shaved in case it was a posh restaurant.

It wasn't so posh as to make them feel uncomfortable, but it had a certain air of classiness. The waiter brought them two glasses of white wine and a small basket of bread and olives to nibble on as they decided on their entrées and mains.

'It's highly suspicious,' Poppy said, enjoying the salty taste of the olives and following it up with a lovely sip of chilled white wine. 'Whoever it was, was after information. Could it be the same person I saw watching the cottages, the night I arrived in Didlinton?'

'Are you saying it was the murderer?' Simon said, his hand frozen half way to spearing another olive with his fork.

'Are you saying that there is a murderer?' Poppy countered. 'Are we really going down that route again? We've only just decided to tell your mum that it's over and we're not going to be detectives any longer.'

'I think I'm starting to think Mum has a point,' Simon said. 'It needs more investigation. We've stirred something up — otherwise why else did someone rummage through my stuff? And it wasn't a common thief or I'd have no tablet, laptop or telly.'

'Someone's scared because we're asking questions. Maybe that same someone was watching your cottage and has gone through your stuff. If that's the case, then I'm a bit creeped out.'

Poppy looked at Simon for reassurance but he wasn't looking back at her. Instead, he was looking over her right shoulder with a horrified expression on his face.

Poppy turned round. A young couple had come in to the restaurant and were waiting to be seated.

'Simon?'

'It's Suzie and Adam,' Simon said faintly.

10

He should be over it all by now, Simon thought. It had been six months since he found out that Suzie was cheating on him with Adam.

Their wedding had been planned for this August. They had got engaged the previous August. He remembered them being so happy together. They were on holiday in Spain when he popped the question. His memory supplied him with snapshots of Suzie's dark hair in the breeze, her laughter and flashing eyes as she said yes, walks in the fresh mountain air and happiness that made his heart want to burst with joy. Adam had slapped him on the back when they got back and insisted on celebrating by throwing them an impromptu engagement party. It was a barbecue at Adam's and all their friends and school colleagues came.

Was that when it happened? Simon was never sure when Suzie and Adam had begun their affair. Was it on that superb summer's day in Adam's garden, replete with hot dogs and beer? Or was it a slow-growing thing, built day by day in the teachers' lounge at school as they ate or marked jotters or moaned about parents' evenings?

Why had Suzie agreed to marry him when she must have known she liked Adam?

Once it became common knowledge at school, it was too painful and humiliating to continue to work there and see Suzie and Adam on a daily basis. He'd handed in his notice and gone back to live with his parents.

At twenty-seven, it was hard living back in his boyhood bedroom. The single bed, the football posters and track medals, the stack of old music CDs and his mum calling him for breakfast had all been difficult.

It had been a relief as well as a surprise to find Mary had left him her cottage. It was a chance to start over, a fresh beginning. His mum was tearful when he left, as if she thought he'd be at home forever. His dad had understood. He'd given Simon a bracing hug.

And now, here were Suzie and Adam in the last place he'd imagined they'd turn up. She couldn't possibly know he was here. He'd told no one at the school and had cut all ties. Didlinton was a seaside town and on the tourist map, so it had to be just a horrible coincidence.

He stared at Suzie. She looked well. Her dark hair was longer and it suited her. The coral dress she was wearing complemented her tanned skin and a gold necklace. She glanced up at Adam and smiled as he said something.

Simon's heart lurched. It was a loving look.

Adam didn't look any different. He'd always had the alpha male aura down to a fine art. He had the classic dark good looks that women adored, strong broad shoulders and a winning smile. He had a charmed life — the only son of wealthy parents, private education and a trust fund. Was that what Suzie had found so appealing?

Simon was also an only child, but had what he thought was a fairly normal upbringing with loving parents and a state school education. He was not wealthy, and as a school teacher was unlikely to be bringing in the millions any time soon. He'd thought love was enough. He'd imagined a life with Suzie, where they built their own family and muddled through like most people.

'Simon?' Poppy whispered, looking concerned.

'It's Suzie and Adam. There,' Simon repeated.

'Your ex-fiancée?' Poppy swivelled in her chair to look.

'Don't,' Simon said, but it was too late.

Suzie and Adam were looking over at them with dawning recognition. The waiter was trying to direct them to a table for two on the far side of the restaurant. Simon was relieved it was far from their table but horrified to see them approaching.

He had heard through mutual friends

174

that they had got married on a beach in Thailand, two months after he and Suzie had split up. That hurt too. Suzie had always told him she wanted a long engagement. Now, he wondered if that was because she had had doubts from the very start.

His heart was pounding so hard he could hear it over the noises in the restaurant. Poppy was speaking, but he didn't hear her over the pulse. People spoke about how annoying tinnitus was. Now he got a flavour of their suffering. It felt as if the pulsing beat might burst out of his ears.

'Simon — is it really you?' Suzie smiled.

He'd forgotten the timbre of her voice. He nearly knocked his wine glass over as he tried to stop his hands trembling. *Be cool, Simon. Show her it doesn't matter any more.*

Except that it did. All the emotions from last year came rushing back. He'd thought he was over it, but he knew now that he wasn't. It hurt so much. It was anger and grief swirling around him like a dense fog no one could penetrate.

And then, Poppy was holding his hand and he stopped trembling. She was speaking and her voice was light and friendly.

'Who's this, darling?' she said.

What? He must have looked as puzzled as he felt, because Poppy kicked him hard under the table. The sudden sharp pain in his shin helped.

'This is Suzie and her . . . husband . . . Adam,' he managed. He sounded normal, he registered with relief.

'I can't believe it's you,' Suzie said, holding her smile and flicking little curious glances between him and Poppy. 'Is this where you moved to after you left the school?'

He saw the wedding ring, gold against her brown skin, and swallowed.

'Simon and I love coming here on holiday.' Poppy smiled. 'Don't we, darling?'

He didn't get a chance to answer because Adam had clearly realised he wasn't a part of the conversation and as alpha male that wouldn't do. He liked to be in charge. It was what made him an excellent teacher — and great at stealing other people's fiancées.

'So, old chap. What a surprise seeing you here. Suzie and I are having a long weekend break before our main holiday in Singapore. We honeymooned there so we'll be revisiting old haunts.'

The best defence is attack, Simon remembered. Adam wasn't apologetic at all. He was rubbing it in Simon's face and Simon was too civilised to do anything about it. In a more primitive era, he might have wrestled Adam to the ground and speared him through. How satisfying. But of course Simon was too decent to do that.

'How lovely,' Poppy gushed and pulled Simon's hand even closer to her. She squeezed it gently. 'Singapore sounds nice, Simon. Should we consider it? Or are you still set on Hawaii?'

'You're getting married?' Suzie said, sounding unsettled. She stared at Poppy.

Adam coughed.

'Let's go, Suze. The waiter's getting impatient —'

Poppy cut across him to answer Suzie, smiling coyly, 'Don't tell anyone, please. We're enjoying it ourselves before we share our good news.'

'Suze!' Adam barked. He pulled at Suzie's arm and she let him lead her away to the table on the far side of the room, glancing back once at Simon and looking unhappy.

Simon slugged his wine down and indicated to the waiter that he wanted another glass.

Opposite him, Poppy looked sympathetic.

'Are you OK?' she asked.

He realised he was still holding her hand. He let it go gently — it felt soft and warm. He could smell her faint flowery fragrance. The restaurant lights glinted off her auburn hair and her green eyes glittered.

'Thank you,' he said simply. 'Although my mum is going to be confused when word of my new engagement gets out via the grapevine.'

Poppy waved that away as if it didn't matter.

'You'll find an excuse for your mum when it's necessary. Right now, it was worth it to see their expressions. How dare they stand there and talk about repeating their honeymoon when they should be afraid to cross your path and should be begging for your forgiveness?' She sounded indignant.

'I can't imagine Adam ever begging anyone for forgiveness.' Simon laughed, and felt a bit better.

'She'll regret marrying him,' Poppy said. 'He's far too bossy. It'll be an unequal marriage. She missed a treasure when she dumped you.'

Simon grinned. 'Don't let Suzie hear you say that. She can be quite bossy too.'

'Lots of clashes waiting to happen, then. I'd rather have a relationship where I've lots in common with my partner and very few arguments.'

'Oh, well,' Simon said, feeling deflated after the surprise encounter. 'I doubt very much if I'll ever have another relationship.'

'Don't say that. You're young — give it a while and you'll meet someone new. Trust me. I felt the same after I split with Alex and I'm not ready yet, but I know I will be at some point.'

The waiter arrived with the main dishes. Simon had thought he'd lost his appetite but when he began to eat, the fish curry was so delicious that he found himself demolishing it all.

Across from him, Poppy tucked into scampi and chips with visible enjoyment. She wasn't a girl who watched her calories, he thought with amusement — and from her slim figure, she didn't need to.

If I was on the lookout for romance, I'd choose Poppy. The thought sprang into his mind unbidden. They got on well as friends, and he felt so comfortable with her. They liked many of the same things. Having chatted about music and theatre and cinema, they'd already jokingly agreed to meet up after the summer to share some of these.

He couldn't help looking across the dimly lit restaurant to where Suzie and Adam were sitting. He couldn't be certain, but it looked as if they were in the middle of a tiff. Suzie was jabbing her finger at Adam and his body language was stiff back and his head pulled back from her. Were they discussing Simon?

After a dessert of tiramisu which was creamy and soaked in marsala wine, they paid the bill and went out into the warm, breezy evening.

'I'm stuffed to the gunwales,' Poppy groaned. 'I should never have had dessert.'

'Me too.' Simon patted his stomach. 'It was a great meal and we didn't talk about Mary and her suspicious demise once, so full marks to us.'

'Except you've mentioned it now,' Poppy joked. 'And the only reason we didn't bring the subject up is because your ex appeared and scuppered the meal.'

Simon was quiet for a moment. He examined his feelings objectively. Yes, it had been a shock seeing Suzie and

Adam and it had brought back all sorts of emotions he'd rather not have experienced again. But, surprisingly, it had been short-lived and he'd enjoyed the rest of the meal with Poppy. She had a store of funny stories about her pupils and although she hadn't travelled much outside the UK, she'd been to many interesting places in Scotland and England.

She was also a good listener and seemed to enjoy hearing about his teaching posts and his gap year experiences.

'Simon?' Poppy said anxiously. 'Sorry, I shouldn't have mentioned Suzie. I know you're upset.'

'I'm not,' he said, honestly. 'Hey, do you fancy a walk along the beach in the dark?'

They walked down the promenade steps on to the sand. Poppy took off her sandals and exclaimed at how cold the sand was.

'Put your shoes back on,' Simon suggested.

'Not on your nelly,' came the response.

'I'm on the beach and I'm going to have a paddle in the sea. Come on, get your shoes off too.'

'I can see that I offered you too much wine with dinner,' Simon teased. 'It's gone to your head.'

'Get them off,' Poppy ordered.

She looked as if she might grapple them off him, so Simon bent down and with a few balancing problems managed to get his shoes and socks off. She was right, the sand was freezing cold on his bare soles. There were no clouds in the sky and the stars twinkled like jewels. A half moon cast some light, and the street lights along the promenade meant they could see where they were going.

Poppy ran down the beach to the sea. It looked black and made rasping sounds as the little waves hit the sand and dribbled back through the pebbles.

'Ahhh, it's cold!' she cried.

'You're not selling it well,' Simon said, staying back from the water and hoping to avoid paddling.

'Seriously, you have to try it. I'm not

doing this by myself.'

Poppy ran back to him and grabbed his hand. She pulled him down to the water's edge where the wavelets lapped and grumbled. They were still holding hands as Simon's feet met the water. He let out a gasp and heard Poppy laugh. It was a freeing sound, and he found himself laughing too. It let out the tension from seeing Suzie and it felt good.

They paddled along, keeping close to the beach. A couple of bats swooped in the air above them, dark silhouettes as they chased insects in the warm air. Simon marvelled that the sea could feel so cold when the air felt warm, but oddly his feet soon felt warm too and he let himself settle into pure sensation and let go of his thoughts.

He saw the bats, the stars and the shape of Poppy in front of him as they paddled. He heard her breathing, the whispering of wings as birds passed overhead and the low rumble of a few cars in the village. He felt the grittiness of sand under his feet, the cool caress of the sea on his ankles where they met the water's surface. He smelled the sand, the sea and Poppy's perfume. He felt . . . at peace.

Poppy stopped at a collection of boats, pulled up on the shore. She went over to one that was an open wooden hull rowing boat with two benches.

'Let's sit in here, shall we? Our feet will dry out.'

He followed her into the boat and they sat side by side on one of the benches.

'I wonder whose boat this is?' he said.

'It's the Isadora, you can see the name painted on the side. It belongs to one of Harry's friends,' Poppy said. 'He won't mind us sitting here. He likes to do a bit of fishing from it and Harry often goes too. Probably that's how Harry caught the enormous fish you helped eat, the day I arrived.'

She wriggled her toes and held her feet up to dry. He noticed how dainty her feet were and how each toenail was painted a pearly pink. Beside her, his feet were large and clumsy and hairy. He wiped his feet on his socks to dry them and put his socks and shoes on, feeling a bit self-conscious. Poppy didn't seem to notice though.

She stretched and yawned.

'Isn't this perfect?'

He looked about at the sea and the sand.

'Yes, it is.'

'You're lucky you're going to live here,' Poppy said, moving about on the bench to get comfortable.

'I'm glad I've made that decision. For a long while I've felt out of control, as if stuff has happened to me and I've had to bend to it. Suzie dumping me and having to live with my parents, losing my job . . . it's been hard. Deciding to live in Mary's — my — cottage has been the first thing I've decided properly in months.'

'Coming to Gilly's for the summer is always magic for me and I never want to go back to Edinburgh and to teaching. But I do — and then I get back into my normal life, and I like it, and I forget all about Didlinton until the next summer.

It's funny, that.'

'Do you think you'd like to live here and work here?' Simon asked, not sure why her answer was important.

She nodded.

'Yes, eventually I'll want to live outside a city.'

She was so close that Simon felt her arm brush against his. It was the lightest of touches and yet it made the tiny hairs on his arm lift up.

If he wanted to, it'd be easy to turn his head and press his lips to hers. He knew he wouldn't. It would change everything. And he liked her company, her friendship. He wasn't going to jeopardise that.

11

It was midnight when Poppy got home. It had been a magical evening, she thought. The food had been wonderful and Simon was excellent company.

He had rallied after the shock of seeing his ex-fiancée and her husband. They had had good fun on the beach. She'd deliberately tried to take his mind off the awful Suzie by taking her sandals off and insisting on going paddling. It had worked.

There was a moment when they were sitting in the Isadora when she thought he might kiss her. Her lips had tingled in anticipation. But he hadn't and then she wondered if she'd imagined it.

Did she want him to? Poppy thought about that. She was perfectly happy being single, as she kept telling herself. She certainly wasn't interested in another relationship like the one she had with Alex. But Simon was different.

She paused before going inside. Unlike Alex, Simon's taste in music and books were very similar to hers. They got on. They had a laugh together. And they were amateur detectives together. She found him very attractive.

All that was enticing enough for Poppy to consider it. The barrier was Simon himself.

It was obvious from this evening that he was not over Suzie. He had been shaking, for goodness' sake, after he saw her. She'd taken his hand to calm him and it had worked. Luckily, she didn't think Suzie had noticed any trembling.

Horrible cow! She didn't deserve Simon anyway. He'd had a lucky escape, in Poppy's opinion.

She went in and smelled cigarette smoke. Of course, Angela was awake. She went in to the living room. Her mother was lounging against the cushions, smoking a roll-up with her eyes screwed shut. She blinked them open as Polly thumped down on an armchair.

'Nice evening?' Angela said, lazily.

'Lovely, thanks. Want a coffee?' Poppy said.

'Too much wine?'

'Not at all. We had a really nice meal and shared a bottle. Mind you, the dessert was heavy on the marsala.'

'Coffee will dilute it then. Make mine black with two sugars, please, sweetie.'

Poppy pushed up off the armchair with difficulty. She'd happily snooze there. She went through to the kitchen and made the coffee. Bringing it back through, she saw Angela had a stack of books beside her.

'Summer reading pile?' She nodded at them.

'Yeah. I've an idea for writing a travelogue, so I'm reading other travellers' tales first. See what the market's like.'

'I thought you wrote travelogues already?'

'I write travel articles. There's a difference. This would be more like a full-length book. Lot of work required.'

'That's impressive,' Poppy said.

Angela laughed. 'I haven't started yet.

Keep the praise until I've actually written it.'

It struck Poppy that she was having a normal conversation with her mother. Like two ordinary people. Two friends, even.

'What do you like about travelling?' she asked. 'I don't see the appeal.'

Angela threw her a mock horrified face.

'That's shocking coming from my own daughter. Travelling is in my blood. It's the freedom, I guess. Making your own decisions on where to go, never having to settle in any one place for long. Always seeing new sights, being stimulated and curious.'

'That's certainly not compatible with being married and having a child,' Poppy said, drily.

Angela sighed. She stubbed out her cigarette and lit another, as if her hands had to be busy.

'Look, I'm sorry. I've been a rubbish mother and I know it. Believe me or not, it's been the greatest regret of my life. I

191

should never have married John and I should never have had children. I'm not suited to it.'

'You left me when I was five. Can you imagine what that does to a small child?' Poppy said.

That normal conversation a few minutes ago had morphed into more usual patterns.

'I'm very selfish. I've accepted that. I chose to go my own path and it was at your expense. Yours and your dad's. I hope you'll forgive me and I hope you've made your own path and that it's a good one.'

'I do like my life.' Poppy sighed. 'But I'd like it better if you were in it. I mean, in a consistent way. So that I know where you are and where you are going to be.'

'This time it'll be different,' Angela said. 'I mean it. I'm renting a house somewhere near here so I can write my book and I'm staying in England permanently. I want to put down roots.'

'What about Dad?'

'He can come and visit. He's always welcome — as are you.'

'Do you really mean it? That you're here for good?' Poppy asked.

'You can come with me to visit the estate agents and be there when he or she hands over the keys. How about that?' Angela smiled.

Poppy wasn't going to hold her breath. There had been promises before and none of them kept. Just when she hoped things would be different, Angela would pack up her bags and disappear. Was it going to be different now?

She realised she didn't know. She'd never know with her mother. That spontaneity was part of Angela's personality, along with her lack of time keeping and her inability to cook. She was flawed, just the same as anyone else. The difference this time was that Poppy was viewing her as another adult, not as the mother she'd needed as a little girl. She was a rubbish mother. They both agreed on that. But maybe she was a better friend?

'Tell me more about your travels in

India,' Poppy said, sinking in to the arm-chair.

The room stank of Angela's cigarette smoke and Poppy vowed to insist on her smoking outside. Tomorrow. She'd tell her tomorrow.

'I'll tell you all about Goa if you really want that, but first I want to talk about us.'

'I'm not sure there is an 'us',' Poppy said. 'You were never there for me as a child and I've learned to live without you. You can't just come back unannounced and decide to be my mother now.'

'I'll always be your mother, whatever happens. But I know I've been a terrible one. I've been selfish and put my own needs first. I'm ashamed of myself. I really am and I wish I could turn back the years and start again. I'll never get that time back with you.'

Poppy was shocked to see Angela crying. She knew she should go and comfort her, but she couldn't. All the residual anger at her mother was still there. Her muscles were stiff with it as

194

she sat in the chair.

'I'm so sorry, Poppy. I'm sorry for everything. If I could go back and do things right, I would. But I can't. Can we please start afresh with each other? It's why I came back to England. I knew from Gilly that you'd be here.'

Poppy couldn't speak. She didn't know where to begin or how she felt.

* * *

The sun was streaming in through the window and the blackbirds in full song when Poppy got up the next day. She pulled her alarm clock round and groaned. It was eleven o'clock. She never slept in. She and Angela had talked until late, although she didn't feel as if anything had been resolved. It was easy for Angela to promise what she liked but action spoke louder than words.

She stumbled through to the shower. After a hot shower and breakfast (or was it lunch?) she felt much better.

195

She walked over to Harry's to check on Tiny. Harry was in his garden with the tarpaulin on his knees, working away at it. Tiny was in a box on the grass beside him, snuggled up to a teddy bear.

'Aw, that's cute,' Poppy said. 'Where did you get the soft toy?'

'One of the kids' from way back. I had to dust it off from the attic and clean it. Stank of moth balls. Tiny's out for the count.'

Poppy knelt by the box. The black and white kitten was curled up asleep, chin and paws on the teddy. He was definitely bigger and his fur was thicker.

'Thanks, Harry. You're doing a fantastic job. Gilly will be so grateful.'

'She's not keeping them all, is she?' Harry asked casually.

Poppy hid a smile as she stroked the kitten. Harry wasn't going to admit his fondness for the small creature.

'She sent me a postcard, delighted about Delilah. She'll be looking for good homes for all five kittens. I don't suppose you know someone who'd take Tiny?

Not everyone wants to have the runt of the litter.'

'I might just hang on to him. Keeps the mice down. Terrible run on the little beggars in the summer.'

'OK. Well, let me know when you decide for sure. I'll let Gilly know.'

Harry stroked the kitten gently. His finger looked giant sized next to the furry body. Tiny stretched and purred, obviously recognising Harry's touch and trusting him. There was a soppy look on the old man's face, which disappeared when he saw Poppy grinning at him.

'What?' he growled.

'Oh, nothing,' Poppy said innocently. 'How's life, anyway?'

'Apart from fishing, swimming and mending this blooming tarpaulin, not much to report. How about you and young Simon? Enjoy your romantic dinner together?'

The glint in Harry's eyes was back.

'How did you . . . oh, I see. You and Angela discussed it, did you? Well, for your information, it was a lovely dinner between friends.'

Now it was Harry's turn to grin knowingly.

'Friends, is it. There's none so blind as will not see, as my dear mother used to say. How's the sleuthing?'

Poppy frowned. 'It's confusing. We were all for giving up as we'd run out of suspects. Then someone went into Simon's home and went through his stuff. We've hit a nerve with someone.

'But we've hit a brick wall. Mary didn't have that many friends, and no other names have come up.'

'I might be able to help you with that,' Harry said mysteriously.

'Oh?'

'Have you spoken to Michael Carmody?' Harry put down the tarpaulin and fixed his gaze on Poppy.

'I've never heard of him. Who is he?'

'He's the chair of the bird watching group. He and Mary were dating for a while earlier in the year.' Harry grinned. 'She bought a lot of new hats around then.'

'Was Mary ever married?'

'I don't think so. She never mentioned a Mr Soull.'

'Tell me more about Michael Carmody. Is he dodgy?'

'Dodgy? Who knows. What I do know is that he was very keen on Mary, and when she ended the relationship, he pestered her. I had to ask him to leave the street once — he'd come visiting and to beg her to go out with him, and he wouldn't go. Mary phoned me and asked if I'd escort him off her doorstep.'

Poppy thought about it.

'So, maybe he was still pestering her and he followed her up the cliff path that morning and when she refused him, he threw her off the path.'

'Isn't that a bit unlikely if he was keen on her?' Harry said. 'Why kill your love?'

'Hell hath no fury like a woman scorned,' Poppy quoted. 'Or, in this case, a man. They do say that love and hate are two sides of the same coin.'

'Mmm.' Harry said, picking up the tarpaulin and pushing the thick needle into it. 'I don't know, but you and young Simon can have fun finding out. And don't forget to tell me all about it.'

'There's a slight problem with your theory about Michael,' Poppy remarked. 'No one reported seeing a man on the cliff path that morning. Simon showed me all the newspaper reports and nothing was mentioned.'

'That doesn't mean anything.' Harry waved the needle dangerously and dismissively. 'Not many people saw Liz up there either or at least, they didn't report it to the police as suspicious. Trust me, you want to speak to Mr Carmody. It can't do any harm, can it?'

* * *

The online phone directory was helpful in providing Michael Carmody's address and number.

'How do we approach him?' Poppy asked Simon. 'What possible reason can we have for speaking to him? This is where it'd be great to be a real detective and then we could flick our official cards at him.'

'You've been watching too many crime series on the telly,' Simon laughed. 'Let's just be honest with him.'

'What, and say 'Hello Mr Carmody — we think you killed Simon's aunt Mary in a crime of passion'?'

Simon shook his head, 'We'll approach him in the same way as Liz and Derek. We just want to know more about Mary's friends.'

'Friends.' Poppy made quote marks in the air.

Simon left the living room and Poppy wondered if she'd offended him. But he returned quickly with a pair of binoculars and three bird books.

'Mary's stuff,' he explained. 'I'm sure she wouldn't mind us using them.'

'OK,' Poppy said, slowly. 'And, we're looking at the stuff because . . . ?'

'Because you and I are going on an excursion with the local bird watching group.' Simon showed her his phone screen. 'There's an outing tomorrow to a local nature reserve — and guess who is leading it?'

'Michael Carmody?'

'Gold star for Poppy. It says here it starts at eleven and we're to bring our own packed lunches. I've booked us on.'

'So, we go on this excursion and somehow get chatting to Michael?' Poppy still wasn't sure how they were going to proceed.

'Yes, if we can. But we can also watch him and see what kind of person he is and I suppose we can try and chat to other group members.'

* * *

The local nature reserve was twenty miles from Didlinton. It was an area of woodlands and meadows with a stream meandering through its centre. Poppy and Simon drove past a wooden sign stating *Grundy Hills Nature Reserve* along a narrow Tarmac road to a small car park. The car park was in the shade, which was pleasant as the sun was hot.

Poppy felt rather sticky with sun cream. She was wearing shorts, a T-shirt, baseball cap and, instead of sandals, had plumped for trainers in case the ground was rough. Simon was wearing trainers too with his jeans and an open-necked blue shirt. The shirt matched his blue eyes, she thought.

Clouds of tiny insects bounced about in the shafts of sunlight through the trees. She waved them away from her face when she got out of the car. There were three other cars in the car park and as she stood there, two more arrived. People emerged from them and it was clear they were all in the bird watching group as they greeted one another.

She counted nine people and added one more as an elderly man wandered back from the path in the woods, wearing a white jacket and sun hat. There was no sign of Liz Soames and she remembered she was away on holiday.

Poppy felt awkward and out of place. She'd borrowed a pair of binoculars from Harry and these hung on a strap around her neck. Harry had told her to bring a notebook and pen for recording birds so she grasped these. In her rucksack she had a packed lunch and a bottle of water, the sun cream tube and a cardigan in case it cooled down later.

Simon grabbed his backpack from the car. She'd brought him a wrapped sandwich and drink for his lunch and he had packed that. He slung the bag over one shoulder, casually, as if used to these excursions. Poppy thought he looked the part much more than she did.

The group had moved together and one man was speaking. Poppy smelled grass and dry earth and the scent of her sun cream, which reminded her of summers past. She nudged Simon and they both moved forward to join the group.

She cast a surreptitious glance around the people present. Most of them were middle-aged or older, and six of them were men. There was one young person, a girl who was dressed like a Goth and had a silver nose-ring. Poppy decided she looked interesting and made a mental note to speak to her.

Simon was staring at the speaker as if fascinated by what he was saying. Earlier, getting ready, Poppy had asked him if he knew anything about birds or bird watching.

'Not a thing,' he'd said blithely. 'But it can't be too hard, can it? I mean there's robins and blackbirds, I can recognise those, and what else is there? Not much. Blue tits maybe.'

She'd been relieved when he said that. Perhaps they'd blend in easily. She had no idea about birds and although she loved hearing the bird song outside the cottage, she hadn't a clue what all the different species were or why anyone would want to spend half a day looking at them.

The speaker stopped as they approached and eyes swivelled towards them as the group registered the newcomers. He had to be the chair, Michael Carmody, she thought. He looked to be in his sixties and had a trim figure and short silver hair. He was quite attractive and she imagined women in their fifties and sixties would like him. He had dark brown eyes, which were now fixed on her and Simon.

'Ahh, we have some visitors to our group today,' he said and his voice was unexpectedly deep and gravelly. 'Hello, I'm Michael and I'm the chair of Didlinton Bird Watching Club. And you are . . . ?'

'Hi everyone, I'm Simon and this is Poppy,' Simon said easily.

'Experts or beginners?' Michael asked, writing their names on a page of his notebook.

'We're beginners but very keen,' Simon said.

'Excellent,' Michael said briskly. 'We can always do with fresh blood in the group. Molly here is our youngest member and brilliant at spotting unusual species. You'll learn a lot. Any birds in particular you're interested in?'

'Oh . . . we're happy to see anything, really.' Poppy smiled and tried to look excited.

'You're in luck today,' Michael said. 'We're likely to see all the usual small woodland passerines plus jay, nuthatch and great spotted woodpecker if we're lucky.'

'Great,' Poppy said.

She had no idea what a passerine was and hadn't heard of nuthatch or jay before. Nervously, she clutched her notebook. At least Simon had said they were beginners so it didn't matter if they showed their ignorance.

'Right, folks.' Michael clapped his hands. 'Off we go. Remember to keep it quiet in the woods and point if you see a bird. No chatting, please.'

Poppy and Simon trooped after the others.

'It's a bit rubbish we can't chat to anyone,' Poppy murmured to Simon. 'That's sort of the whole point of the exercise.'

The old man in the white jacket who was walking just in front of them turned and frowned. He made a show of putting his finger over his lips to indicate silence before walking on.

Poppy made a face. Simon grinned at her and they followed the others into the woods.

12

It was quiet in the woods — apart from the noises of the club members' feet on the wood chip path and the songs of the birds.

In fact, it wasn't quiet at all, Poppy thought incredulously. If you listened to the birds, it was a cacophony of sound, a real din.

Beside her, Simon fumbled with his binoculars trying to focus the lenses. The old man in the white jacket kept stopping and staring at the tree tops. A couple of times, Poppy had almost stumbled into him.

Ahead, Michael looked excited and jabbed his finger at a tall, willowy tree. The bird watchers all pointed their binoculars at it. Simon did the same.

Poppy found herself struggling with hers. The view was fuzzy and she wasn't able to see the tree, let alone the birds.

'Want a hand with that?' someone whispered.

She looked around to see Molly beside her.

'I can focus them for you,' the girl offered.

Gratefully, Poppy handed the binoculars over and Molly did some swivelling of parts of them before giving them back.

'What's in the tree?' Poppy asked, keeping her voice low to prevent Mr White Jacket from complaining.

'It's a Tree Creeper,' Molly said. 'Can you see it spiralling up the trunk of the tree?'

Poppy tried to see through the binoculars. After a moment she did see it. A small brown bird with a pure white breast was creeping up the bark of the tree. She brought the binoculars down and let them hang from their strap. Molly was still watching the bird and the rest of the group were too, except for Simon, who was standing looking bored.

Poppy threw him a meaningful glare. He tried to look interested.

Actually, she was beginning to enjoy herself. The Tree Creeper was a pretty little creature and now she had control of the binoculars, things were looking up.

They all moved on. It was nice to get a walk outside and to be in a group of enthusiastic people, even if she wasn't very good at any of this.

'You can write that on your birding list,' Molly said, hanging back to walk beside her.

Simon had moved on to walk with a couple ahead and despite Michael Carmody's command to be quiet, most people were chatting quietly. Simon was in conversation with the couple and Poppy hoped he was finding out useful information.

'My birding list? Oh, yes, of course,' Poppy obediently wrote 'Tree Creeper' on the fresh page of her notebook.

'I've got a daily list, a weekly count and a life list,' Molly informed her proudly.

'So, what's the attraction? I don't mean to be rude but you're an awful lot younger than the rest of the group.'

Molly shrugged. 'I'm considered weird by my friends 'cos I like birds. This lot, they don't judge me. I like seeing new birds and adding them to my lists.'

'It must be good having experts to help you learn,' Poppy said, trying to bring the conversation round to Michael Carmody without being too obvious. 'Who's the best at this sort of thing?'

'At birding?' Molly said, sounding amused at Poppy's vagueness. 'Mr Carmody, of course.

'That's the chairman?' Poppy didn't want to appear to know of him.

'Yeah. He's amazing. I mean, he's like a grandad to me and he's taught me so much. He gave me my first bird book when he knew I was interested.'

'Do you have other hobbies?' Poppy asked. This wasn't relevant to their investigation but she was curious why a fifteen-year-old wanted to spend a morning with older people.

'Yeah, sure. I'm really into music like all my friends — and fashion, as you can see. Watching birds, though — no one wants to do that.'

Poppy understood that. It wasn't a hobby that most young people were involved in.

They walked on together until the group stopped to look at another bird. She took the opportunity to shuffle round near Simon. He hadn't even raised his binoculars this time.

'When's lunch, do you think?' he whispered to her.

'You can't be hungry. You had a huge breakfast.'

'Walking brings on an appetite. But, actually, I was thinking that lunch is the perfect chance to ask about Michael.'

'Good idea.' Poppy nodded. 'Let's split our forces and report back after. Right now we need to look at that tree, we're attracting funny looks.'

They both raised their binoculars in the rough direction of everyone else's. Catching Michael Carmody's stare, Poppy pretended to write in her notebook.

After what seemed like an interminable while later, a lunch break was announced. By now, they had left the woodlands and walked beside a small stream into flower meadows. In the middle of the meadows were a couple of picnic benches and some fallen logs for sitting on.

They spread out. The group opened rucksacks and produced sandwiches, flasks, packets of crisps and other snacks. Poppy sat at one of the picnic benches with two of the other women.

Michael Carmody came up to her. He didn't sit but stood with his hands in his pockets.

'Are you enjoying the excursion?'

His dark brown eyes bored into hers and made her feel uncomfortable, as if he could see straight through her.

'Yes, it's great,' she said with a smile.

'So do you and your partner live locally?' he asked.

'Oh, he's not my . . . No, we're visiting Didlinton on holiday. We thought we'd try something different while we're here,'

Poppy improvised, hoping Simon would tell a similar story if asked.

'What do you do for a living?'

Now it felt as if she was the one being interrogated and investigated. She didn't like it at all. Why was he so curious? Was he suspicious of them? And if he was, why did he feel he had a reason to be? Was it a case of a guilty conscience?

'We're teachers. Nature and outdoor learning are part of the curriculum so it's nice to experience it ourselves before teaching it,' she said truthfully.

In fact, the bird watching had opened her eyes to an activity she thought her pupils might enjoy next school term. They could even have a bird table in the school grounds and see which small birds came to visit. The kids would love it.

'Righty-oh. Enjoy your lunch. That's certainly a doorstepper,' he commented, looking at her lunch.

He went off to the next picnic bench where some of the men were sitting. They bunched up to make space for him.

Poppy looked at her ham salad sandwich. It was Harry's lettuce that made it so bulky. The sandwich was enormous. She took a bite and it was delicious. She had a bottle of lemonade and a packet of spring onion flavour crisps. The other two women had ham rolls and small packets of mixed nuts and were sharing a flask of tea.

'Would you like some?' one of them asked with a kind smile, lifting the flask.

'Thank you but I'm fine,' Poppy said. She was glad of a way in to their conversation. It was clear they were good friends from the way they had been chatting. 'Are the excursions a regular meeting?'

The woman with the flask, who had a short grey bob and wore a thin pink fleece over three quarter length jeans, answered.

'Yes, there's one every month. Jean and I come to most of them, don't we?'

Jean who had long, faded fair hair and pale blue eyes, nodded in agreement.

'We do, indeed. Wouldn't miss them

216

for the world, they're such fun. You missed the February outing, didn't you, Shirley? You had the flu then. But apart from that, we make them all. Michael is such a wonderful leader and so very knowledgeable.'

Shirley smiled at Poppy. 'You're so lucky to experience one of our outings. As Jean says, Michael is a real whizz when it comes to birds. He knows everything, I'm not exaggerating. You can ask what you like and he'll know the answer. And such a nice man. He's never too busy to help if you're struggling with an identification.'

'Is he married?' Poppy asked, hoping this might bring Mary Soull into the conversation.

She got a surprise, therefore, when Jean gave her answer.

'He's got a lady friend over in the town. She came to one of the social evenings recently. A Hilda Greenburg. Lovely lady, and American, I think.'

'No, Jean. She's Canadian. I remember her telling me that,' Shirley said. 'She's not interested in bird watching but he met her at a bridge party. That's Michael's other passion.'

'Have they been together long?' Poppy asked, desperately.

Harry had said Michael Carmody was fixated on Mary Soull. Why then was he dating this Hilda Greenburg? It didn't make sense.

Both Jean and Shirley stared at her. Poppy flushed and made a big deal out of unscrewing her bottle of lemonade and taking a sip. She sounded far too interested in Michael's love life. Her next bite of sandwich clogged in her throat and she swallowed the lump down with a cough.

'Sorry, I'm naturally nosy,' she laughed apologetically. 'My Mum's always telling me curiosity killed the cat.'

They both laughed and seemed more relaxed. Poppy blew out a silent breath of relief.

Shirley turned to Jean. 'They got together at the summer conference, didn't they?'

Jean nodded. 'That's right. We had

conference room A for the bird watching and the bridge lot had conference room B. Michael, being interested in bridge, had nipped in at lunchtime to see what they were doing and met Hilda there.'

'Did you know Mary Soull well?' Poppy asked, trying a different tack. 'Simon is her nephew.'

'Oh, dear. I'm sorry for his loss, it was a dreadful business,' Jean said sincerely. 'We both knew Mary. She came to all the meetings and excursions.'

'She wasn't an easy person to get to know,' Shirley said. 'She didn't say much about her personal life. She was a good friend of Michael's. They both had a similar level of knowledge about birds and had many discussions.'

Mary and Michael were good friends, Poppy mused. If they had been dating, it wasn't obvious to the people who knew them in this group. They had kept it quiet.

'OK, folks, let's tidy up and walk back round the loop. There's a buzzard's nest I want to show you,' Michael boomed out from the other picnic bench.

Everyone began to stow their lunch remains in their rucksacks. Poppy looked ruefully at her packet of crisps. She'd have to eat them later. Shirley and Jean smiled at her but left the bench together, heads together and chatting. Poppy took her cue. She wasn't invited to walk with them.

Still, she'd managed to get some information and hoped that Simon had too. He had taken a spit on one of the logs to eat but then circulated, chatting to the men sitting at the second picnic bench. He looked relaxed and at ease.

She couldn't speak to him as everyone was silent as they walked along the path towards the buzzard nest. They were on a loop path through the nature reserve, which eventually took them back to the car park via a fringe of woodland.

The buzzard nest was impressively large, and a buzzard was helpfully perched on top of it. Even Poppy could see it easily through the binoculars, it was such a big bird. Its beak and talons looked sharp and she pitied any small creature in the grasslands when it was hunting.

Molly grinned at her with excitement and she smiled back. The buzzard's nest was quite an amazing sight and she felt quite privileged to view it. She caught Michael Carmody staring at her and avoided meeting his eyes.

Eventually they made their way back to the car park, by which time Poppy was tired from the heat and the walking. She had enjoyed herself, though, and had decided to buy a children's book about birds to share with her class.

She took a moment to speak to Shirley and Jean. Then she said goodbye to Molly. They waved goodbye to everyone else and called their thanks. Poppy sank gratefully into the passenger seat of Simon's car.

'That was fun but thank goodness it's finished,' she gasped, fanning her hot face with her notebook. 'I'm boiled, and I'm dying for a glass of water. I drank my lemonade about two hours ago.'

'It was a long outing,' Simon agreed, reversing carefully out of the car parking space and driving homeward. 'Shall we go to Katie's Diner for drinks?'

'Ahhh — lovely.'

* * *

Katie's Diner was busy, but they managed to get the last table. It was a small table with two chairs, so they didn't need to worry about having to share and have somebody overhear their conversation. Simon bought two pint glasses of lemonade and brought them over. Poppy rummaged in her rucksack and produced her slightly squashed bag of crisps. She opened the packet for them to share.

'What did you find out about Michael?' she asked, after a long gulp of cold lemonade.

'All the other men find him either overbearing, over confident or downright bossy.'

'If they feel like that, then why don't

222

they vote for a different chair person?'

Simon helped himself to some crisps and frowned.

'Probably because as in any community group, there's lots of grumbling but only a few people who actually volunteer to be the chair or treasurer or secretary. They tolerate Michael because he's good at organising the meetings, but they don't have to like it — or him.'

Poppy smiled admiringly.

'You're quite the pop psychologist, aren't you.'

Simon grinned. 'Or I've been in a couple of organisations and know the score.'

'Well, the women think he's wonderful,' Poppy said. 'He's nice and helpful and extremely knowledgeable. How strange they've such a different perspective.'

'Is it? I suppose the women might find him attractive and that might colour how they find him.'

'True. Anyway, we've got a bigger problem than that,' Poppy said.

'And what's that?'

'Jean and Shirley told me how Michael

had met his partner, Hilda, at their summer conference. So that means he wasn't interested any more in Mary which takes away a motive for killing her in a jealous rage. Also, in the car park at the end, I thought to ask them when the summer conference took place. Guess when?'

'The weekend before the seventeenth of June?' Simon guessed with a sigh.

Poppy nodded. 'Yes, the very same — except it was a long weekend so it ran from the Friday to the Monday afternoon. Lots of people saw Michael Carmody there so he has plenty of alibis. He couldn't have murdered Mary because he was in Bournemouth.'

'We're back to the start again,' Simon groaned.

'It looks like it. But there's something fishy about that guy. Harry told me Mary phoned him because Michael was pestering her, and Harry had to escort him away from her cottage and the street. We need to find out more about that.'

'I don't know,' Simon said. 'Maybe we should leave it. We've done enough to satisfy my mother.'

'We can't leave it,' Poppy argued. 'I want to know about Mary and Michael. Besides, we still don't know who was watching your cottage — and who broke in and what they were looking for.'

Simon rubbed his eyes. He looked hot and tired. His empty glass was on the table and the crisp packet was empty but for a few crumbs.

'I'm going home,' he said.

'Oh — OK, I'll see you later,' Poppy said.

She ordered another drink, annoyed at Simon. He was giving up too easily. Someone out there knew what had happened to Mary, she was convinced of it. Most likely the person who had watched where Simon lived and then gone through his stuff.

Then she felt bad. It was the nearest she and Simon had come to an argument. He had gone off stiff-backed, and there had been a definite atmosphere between them.

They had become such good friends

in a short time that it was odd to disagree with him. She didn't like it; it made her feel uneasy and out of sorts.

She drank some of her lemonade but it went down the wrong way making her choke. She coughed and spluttered. Mopping her front where the liquid had splashed, she didn't notice a shadow over her for a moment. A man sat down opposite her.

She looked up, ready to say that the table was taken, and was shocked into silence. Michael Carmody sat there — and his face was furious.

'You've been asking people about me,' he snarled. 'What's this all about?'

Poppy's heart beat fast in her chest. She clasped her hands together under the table to give herself strength. Her gaze flicked around. At least they were in a public place. He was hardly likely to attack her. Gradually her shoulders came down. She was being ridiculous. He was angry and perhaps he had a right to be. She had been snooping, and so had Simon.

'I'm sorry,' she said.

It seemed to deflate his anger and he calmed. He put his arms on the table and stared at her.

'What were you doing?'

There was no point in lying. Poppy told him the truth. How they were trying to find out if Mary's death was suspicious. What Harry had told her about him and Mary. All of it.

At the end of her slightly rambling confession, Michael gave a large sigh and leaned his forehead onto his arms. She had an unnerving view of a small bald patch on his head before he sat up straight again.

'Yes, I was fond of Mary and yes, we did go on a few dates. I thought I was in love with her. But she didn't feel the same for me. I made a fool of myself. There's nothing like an old fool, as they say. I couldn't take no for an answer and I pleaded with her to go out with me. The day you mentioned, when Harry got involved, I had gone to see her to apologise. I had met someone else and realised my behaviour towards Mary had been pretty embarrassing.

'She wouldn't see me. I was leaving when Harry came. She'd phoned him. It was unnecessary as I was leaving anyway.'

'You'd met someone else?'

'Yes — I'd met Hilda at a bridge party and we had a lot in common.'

'This was before the summer conference? Only, Shirley and Jean told me you got together with Hilda then.'

Michael gave a dry laugh. 'I don't need a diary, do I? Those two biddies have my life covered. They're wrong, as it happens. I already knew Hilda and we were dating. I sneaked into the bridge conference at lunchtime to see her, but it wasn't the first time I saw her. Your information is incorrect.'

He stood up, blocking Poppy's sunshine. She shivered in his cast shadow.

'I don't want to see you or your partner at our bird meetings.' He spoke evenly.

'That's fair enough,' she said. 'We won't bother you again. And I am sorry, for what it's worth.'

She watched him stride away before she headed off in the opposite direction, taking a circuitous route home around the edge of the village.

She hesitated outside Simon's gate, wanting to tell him about her confrontation with the bird watching chairman, but then she gave herself a shake, walked on and let herself into Gilly's cottage.

It was cool and peaceful in the hallway. She breathed in the scent of lavender and wondered what would happen next.

13

Simon received a letter the next day. It had been sent to his parents' address and they had redirected it unopened.

When he slit the envelope open there was a letter from Suzie, written on lilac-coloured, scented paper. When he saw her handwriting, he had to sit down. He stared at the paper, not seeing the words and remembering the shock of meeting her and Adam so recently.

He made a coffee to fortify himself before reading it. When he finished it, he wondered why she had bothered to write. Until he read it again and then he thought he understood.

It was a short letter, and started with her saying how she didn't know his address so she was sending it to his parents' home and hoping they would send it on to him. She went on to say how lovely it had been to see him in Didlinton and that she and Adam were pleased he had obviously moved on with his life.

That part angered him. What did she know about moving on? He had torn up his whole life in an attempt to get over her.

The letter went on that she hoped he could find it in his heart to forgive them, and that she wouldn't bother him again if he didn't want to keep in contact. But just in case, she included their new address so he could write, and her email address if he wanted to send anything.

Simon put the note down on the kitchen table where it loomed large in his vision. On first reading, it seemed inane and bland, like a letter one was forced to write to an elderly relative after Christmas. But on a second reading, he read between the lines and felt her loneliness.

She needed him. Perhaps marriage to Adam wasn't as fantastic as she'd hoped it would be. Why else would she want to stay in touch with Simon?

It unsettled him. He got his laptop and switched it on. He went to his emails and his finger hovered over the keyboard.

In the end, he didn't write to her. He put on his jacket and slammed the gate behind him as he headed to the beach.

He walked for ages along the soft sands towards the headland in the far distance, the opposite direction from the secret beach where Brandon Tulloe took his lovers.

He tried to analyse his feelings. He realised he wasn't excited to get Suzie's letter. He'd been shocked to receive it but once the shock waned, he felt . . . nothing.

There was no reason to keep in touch with her. That part of his life was over. However, he no longer felt distraught. Instead, he felt a vague sadness for his former self. He had enjoyed his job in the north-east, and he'd enjoyed being in love with Suzie.

He wasn't in love with her any more. Simon stood stock still, his heels sinking into the sand. It was true. He didn't love her. He felt as if a weight lifted from his shoulders.

If there hadn't been other people on

232

the beach, he might have lifted up his arms and screamed his freedom. As it was, he contented himself with a low whoop and kicking some pebbles into the sea.

The trouble was, he now admitted he was falling in love with someone else. He hadn't given himself any space to breathe. Poppy Johnson had jumped cheerfully into his life and under the shrub in his garden without so much as a by-your-leave.

He'd been instantly attracted to her physically. He could ignore that. There were plenty of attractive women in the world. But her friendship — that was different. The more he spent time with her, the more he realised how kind and generous and caring she was.

Now, he kicked more pebbles into the waiting wavelets but these were more vigorous as they fell through the air. He couldn't be in love. He mustn't be in love. The timing was all wrong. He needed space to be himself. He needed to be alone to sort his life out.

But Poppy was always there. Just next door if he needed a chat, or popping round to chat about their sleuthing.

It had to stop. He had to tell her that.

He stopped at Katie's Diner on the way back and bought a coffee and a doughnut. Katie, a gruff, stout woman who never spoke much, asked him where his wife was. Simon's mouth opened and closed.

Katie grunted, took his money and pointed at an empty table. Simon sat with his drink and food, but he hardly tasted it.

That was the problem. They were so comfortable together, they got on so well, that it felt natural to spend days together. At the end of the summer, Poppy would go back to Edinburgh and her real life and he would be alone again.

Which was what he wanted, right? Simon didn't know. But he did know he couldn't deal with more heartbreak. What if he acted on his feelings for Poppy and she didn't return them? Or was it worse if she did return them? What if she was looking for a summer romance only?

He went back to his cottage and into the back garden, restless. Two of Gilly's cats were sunbathing on his patio, a fluffy ginger monster and the fat black and white one with an enormous tail. Neither acknowledged him as they soaked up the heat.

He stepped over them to reach the tiny lawn. He changed his mind, and went down the strip beside the house and over to Gilly's.

Poppy answered the door with a wide smile of delight which only made him feel worse. She was wearing shorts, a T shirt and a pair of gloves.

'Simon, I was just thinking about you. I'm out in the back garden weeding, come on through.'

He squeezed past the dresser in the hall and managed to avoid a row of shoes and Wellingtons and a carved wooden crane. Gilly didn't believe in wasting space in her home. Poppy was humming a little tune and he felt bad, knowing he was about to destroy her good mood.

There was a heap of weeds on the tiny patio and a gardening fork left carelessly, prongs up, beside it. Simon turned it over to prevent accidents. Poppy sank down onto one of the outdoor iron seats and motioned for him to do the same. He sat gingerly.

'Michael Carmody found me yesterday,' she said. 'At Katie's Diner. He was furious that we'd been checking up on him. I had to explain what we were up to and apologise. Having heard what he had to say, I think he's innocent.'

'Look, Poppy — I want to stop this.'

'What do you mean?'

'Exactly that,' he said, impatiently, 'We tried to look into anyone who might have been with Mary when she died and everyone has an alibi. Her death was accidental. It's clear now.'

'It's not clear,' Poppy protested, her smile wavering. 'OK, we've investigated Brandon Tulloe, Liz and Derek and now Michael Carmody but what if we've missed someone?'

Simon shook his head.

236

'We're not detectives. This isn't some game we're playing. My poor aunt slipped off that cliff and died. End of story.'

'But Simon, what about the person I saw watching your cottage? What about the break-in?'

'You might have been mistaken about the person. It was probably someone out for an evening walk who'd stopped to tie a shoelace or take in the view or catch their breath. I don't know,' Simon said.

'And the break-in?'

'It was hardly a break-in as I'd left the front door unlocked. Maybe I imagined it. After all, nothing was missing.'

Poppy stood up so abruptly that the gardening gloves fell off her lap where she'd put them.

'I don't believe that. And neither do you, really. Someone was in your cottage looking for something. Why are you denying that? What's going on, Simon?'

'Nothing's going on, as you put it.' Simon's voice rose in the same way Poppy's had. They were in danger of shouting at each other so he deliberately lowered his tone. 'It's over, OK? I'm going to tell my mother that we looked into it and there's nothing suspicious about my aunt's death.'

'There's something else, isn't there?' Poppy persisted, staring intently at him. 'What's wrong?'

He couldn't meet her gaze. He could hardly tell her that he was falling in love with her and that he couldn't do that. He just couldn't.

He needed to run away and put space between them. He had to sort himself out. And that meant being alone to do so. If he spent more time with her, playing detectives, he'd only fall further.

'There's nothing wrong, don't be ridiculous,' he said sharply.

She looked wounded by his sharpness and he felt rotten.

'Look,' he went on, 'You said Michael Carmody was furious that we'd been snooping. He was right to be. It's wrong of us to stir up people's private lives and their secrets. We're not the police. We're two people on holiday. Don't you want to enjoy the summer? It's not long until Gilly is back and you're heading north to the new semester of school.'

There was a horrible silence. Poppy picked up the gardening gloves and put them on the table.

'OK, if that's the way you feel, then we'll end it now,' she said, stiffly. 'I'll show you out.'

Why did it feel as if it wasn't simply the sleuthing that was ending? He had dealt with this badly, but he didn't know how to make it right.

Poppy's expression was closed. He couldn't bear it. He was used to her happy smile and sparkling green eyes looking at him. He'd hurt her but he didn't know how to make it better.

'Poppy . . .' he began.

'See you later, Simon,' she said coolly, opening her front door. 'I hope you enjoy the rest of the summer.'

Simon opened his mouth but didn't know what to say. Anything to bring back the Poppy he knew and loved.

It was no good. He mumbled a good-bye and left without looking back.

★ ★ ★

Poppy walked out of the village and along the track that led to the cliff path. She climbed over the stile into the fields and followed the main path.

The argument with Simon had been horrible. She was only glad that Angela hadn't been in to hear it. She didn't understand what had happened to change his mind. They were so close to finding out what had happened to Mary. They had eliminated a few suspects and were stumped just now, but someone knew more than they had let on, Poppy was certain of it. She wanted to go back over everything that they'd found out and everyone they'd spoken to.

It was frustrating that Simon wanted to finish it. What was more upsetting was that they had shouted at each other. It was their first real disagreement. Simon had asked if she wanted to enjoy the

240

summer and the last weeks of being in Didlinton. How could he not understand that she *was* enjoying it?

She was enjoying being with him.

The fact was, she was in love with him.

Wow, where had that come from? Poppy stopped on the dusty track and considered her own thoughts.

It was true. She fancied him like crazy and had done since he'd first brandished a rolling pin at her. But it was more than that. She had got to know him over the last few weeks and they liked many of the same things, had lots of laughs together and she simply liked being with him. He was gentle and considerate but his intense blue eyes suggested passion too.

I'm in love with Simon, she thought, wonderingly. Which meant that their argument was actually their first lovers' tiff.

Poppy grinned to herself and then felt sad all over again. What was wrong with him? Why had he suddenly decided to give their investigation up? And give her up too, it seemed? She sighed and scuffed her dusty trainers on the path.

Oh dear. She'd pretty much told him not to come round again when she showed him the door. Only, she'd been furious with him.

'I'll invite him round for a meal,' she told herself out loud. 'That's what I'll do. He likes fish. I'll ask Harry to catch me a lovely fresh fish and I'll even gut it and cook it. He won't be able to resist.'

Cheered by that thought, she walked more swiftly up the track to the cliff path. She was almost at the point where the lower path split off and became chalky and crumbly. There were a few dog walkers and couples on the main track but she noticed they were all walking up to the headlands and the flat grassy tops of the cliffs. There was no one on the lower path.

'Hey ho, off we go,' she said to herself cheerfully. 'It's fine. One foot in front of the other, Poppy Johnson. That will do it.'

Talking to herself sometimes helped when she was nervous or anxious. She wasn't sure it was working now. At some point along the walk, she'd decided to keep looking into Mary Soull's death, whatever Simon said.

It wasn't in her nature to give up on things. That included Simon. She wasn't going to let him go on an argument. A meal would fix them up. She might not tell him she was still sleuthing. At least, until she had something proper to report.

The lower path was as crumbly as before. How had Liz Soames described it? Chossy. That was the word. Poppy had never heard of it until then but she felt it described the path perfectly.

Her feet slipped slightly despite the grip of her rubber soles. Her heart missed a beat in panic. With relief she saw the alcove with its wooden bench come into view. She sat on it, hoping to calm down.

The view to the private beach was clear on this sunny day. Little white clouds floated in an otherwise blue sky. The beach below looked golden brown and the sea was a glossy, syrupy green.

There was no private yacht today. Sea birds flew above the sea's surface and dipped below the water to catch fish. It really was idyllic, she thought idly. She heard her own breathing, the distant lapping of the sea, the cries of the birds and the gritty noises of the chalk under her trainers as she moved her feet.

The silence became uneasy. She wished for other people to appear along the path. The tiny hairs on the back of her neck prickled as if someone was watching her. That primitive sixth sense that modern humans like to sneer at as imagination, but that had saved many primitive lives in the distant past.

Poppy turned in each direction, her fingers gripping the warm wood of the bench. There was no one there. So why did she have the intense sensation that she was not alone?

There was a tiny sound behind her. She gasped and moved round. A trickle of stones came from the cliff above her. Someone was up there.

At that very moment, her mobile

phone rang.

The sound was loud and out of place and shrill. She fumbled in her pocket for her phone and managed to answer it before it went to voicemail.

'Hello?' Her voice quivered. She still stared up at the cliff, straining to see who had unwittingly sent the pebbles raining down. Who had been watching her? Following her?

'Hi, Popps. It's Alex here. How're you doing?'

'Alex?' She was momentarily dizzy. He was out of place here, in this place of danger. 'Why are you phoning?'

'Yeah, it's been a while. Thought I'd give you a bell, see if you wanted to hang out tonight? There's a group of us going to Macks for beers if you wanna join us?'

'Alex, I'm not in Edinburgh. I'm down in Didlinton. I always come here for the summers, remember?' Poppy said.

'Ahhh, I forgot. Oh well, another time, yeah?' He closed the call before she could say goodbye.

Poppy stared at her phone and then

shook her head. Weird. She hoped Alex wasn't trying to ask her out on a date to rekindle their disastrous relationship. It wasn't going to happen.

She put a block on his number and pushed the phone back into her shorts pocket. She got up and walked back along the path to the main track. Whoever had been there was long gone, she knew that instinctively.

When she got back to Gilly's cottage, there was a postcard in the hallway that had been slipped under the door. It had a picture of a cat on it. Simon's writing was on the back. She read it. He'd gone home to his parents for a few days.

14

Poppy opened the fridge and looked inside. There was the remains of a lettuce, two cheeses, milk and butter and a half-used jar of curry paste. There was nothing to make a meal with.

She was hungry but didn't know what she wanted to eat. The thought of having to go shopping made her groan. She was out of sorts. She missed Simon and he'd only been gone a couple of hours.

She shut the fridge door to find Bubbles staring at her.

'I can at least feed you,' she said.

Bubbles kept staring as if to say, *Well, get on it with it then*. Poppy made a face but went obediently to the cupboard where Gilly kept the cat food and drew out a pouch. As soon as she'd emptied it into Bubbles' bowl, Geoffrey and Delilah appeared. She fed them too and felt as if she'd achieved something.

She wandered round the cottage,

which didn't take long. Without making a decision, she found herself going out and round to Harry's.

There was a strong smell of fresh fish as she let herself in through the open door. She heard merry whistling and went in to the kitchen. Harry was gutting fish at the sink. Tiny was in his box on the kitchen table.

'Harry?' Poppy called, not wanting to surprise him. Harry turned, a large mackerel in one hand, and grinned. 'Hello, my lovely. Fancy a fish dinner, do you?'

'If you're offering,' Poppy said, hopefully.

'Get yourself a knife and peel the tatties. Know how to make oven chips?'

'I don't, but I'm a quick learner.' She grinned back at him, feeling happier already.

Harry's old radio was on the table and he told her to put it on and find a decent station with good music. In Harry's book, that was jazz, so Poppy found some. It was amazingly soothing and she hummed along as she peeled the potatoes and put them on to boil. Tiny slept through the noise and activity cuddled into his teddy bear.

On instruction from Harry, she went outside into his garden to pick a lettuce and some snap peas. She noticed the tarpaulin was patched and folded.

When the potatoes were boiled, Harry showed her how to cut them into chips, cover them in oil and bake them in the oven.

'Much healthier and tastier than fried chips,' he said, sliding the mackerel fillets under the grill. 'Now, get that salad chopped and we're on the way to the best supper possible.'

They ate outside in the garden, leaving Tiny in possession of the kitchen table. Harry was right, the meal was delicious. Poppy scraped up every last bit from her plate and had to stop short of licking it.

'Had a spat with young Simon, have you?' Harry said conversationally as they drank coffee afterwards with the evening sun still warm on their backs.

'What makes you say that?' Poppy said defensively.

'I imagine you'd rather spend a lovely summer's evening having a meal with your boyfriend than an old grump like me.'

'There's a lot wrong with that statement. Firstly, he's not my boyfriend and secondly you are not an old grump. I love spending time with you. And you make the best food ever,' she added.

'That's as maybe, but you and Simon have had a falling out.'

'Fine, yes, we have. He's gone home to see his parents. We argued about Mary. He doesn't want to look into her accident any more, but I do. What do you think we should do?'

Harry rubbed his nose and took a moment to answer.

'As it's Simon's aunt, I'd say it's his call. Maybe he's right and it's time to put all that nosing around to bed. After all, what've you found out?'

Poppy was dismayed that Harry was taking Simon's side.

'We've established alibis for people we suspected. That's something. Someone knows more about Mary's death than they're letting on. I'm sure of it. I went up to the cliff path today and I'm certain someone was watching me. If I hadn't got a phone call, I wonder what would've happened.'

'Someone was watching you?' Harry sounded concerned now.

'Yes. They were up on the top of the cliff above where I was sitting. It could've been walkers, but I know it wasn't. Whoever it was, was watching me. I felt it.'

'Then I'd say it was definitely time to stop your nosing around. Simon's right.'

'But to stop now when we're getting close?' Poppy cried, 'I can't. I have to know.'

Harry put a large hand over hers.

'I'm very fond of you, Poppy girl. I don't want to see anything bad happen to you. Gilly would never forgive me. You need to stop. Promise me?'

Poppy gave a sigh. She was being

ganged up on. First Simon and now Harry.

'OK, I promise. I'll stop looking for suspects.'

Harry sat back, looking satisfied.

'That's my girl. Enjoy your summer and relax.'

Poppy stood up. 'I'll do the washing up. It was a great dinner, thanks.'

Harry got up. 'We cooked it together so we'll wash up together. And Poppy . . .'

'Mmm?'

'Young Simon is very, very fond of you. I've seen the way he looks at you. Don't mess it up. Make up your quarrel.'

★ ★ ★

Angela wasn't in when Poppy went back to Gilly's that evening. She felt happier especially when she thought of Harry's words. Simon was fond of her. More than fond.

Before she could sit down in the living room she had to pick up Angela's clothing and books. She brushed away crumbs from the cushions and took an ashtray into the kitchen to rinse it out. There was a stale smell of smoke so she opened the windows for a breeze and fresh air.

Finally, she was able to sit down and watch the television in comfort. Honestly, it felt as if she was the adult and her mother was a lazy teenager. She certainly didn't clean up after herself.

They didn't share meals either, as their schedules were so different. Poppy liked to get up early and make the most of the day, which meant that by eleven at night she was more than ready for her bed.

Angela, on the other hand, tended to surface at midday and then stay up until three or four in the morning. Poppy often heard the television murmuring as she lay in bed trying to sleep. A couple of times she'd got up and complained until Angela turned the sound down. She'd stomped back to bed, wondering when her mother would leave Gilly's and give her peace.

She thought about Simon. How long was he going to be away? She read his postcard again looking for clues. It said *Going home to my parents for a few days.* He'd signed his name at the bottom. Not even a love from. Just his name.

She propped the postcard up on the low coffee table in front of the sofa so she could see it as she watched the telly.

She must've fallen asleep because she was woken by the slam of the front door and a cold draught as Angela breezed in. The telly was still on, showing a woman in a haunted house being stalked by a killer.

'You still up, sweetie?' Angela threw herself down onto the sofa, making Poppy jump.

Her mother was accompanied by the smell of garlic and cigarettes. She was wearing an old Indian cotton purple skirt that reached her ankles and a beaded top. Her long hair streamed down her back. She wore no make-up, but Poppy thought she looked younger than her years and healthier than when she'd first arrived.

'Where were you?' she asked, sounding like a concerned parent whose teenage daughter had defied curfew and come home too late.

'I met a few friends for a curry. Then we had a beer or two and a walk in the dark across the beach. It was really nice.' Angela yawned and stretched. 'Want a cuppa?'

'Yes, please.' Poppy gave up on sleep and watching telly. She turned the box off. 'Go on, I'll make it.'

'Great. Two sugars and lots of milk in mine.'

Poppy came back with the tea to find Angela lying on the couch. With a sigh, she handed over the tea and sat in the armchair.

'What friends?' she asked.

'Hmm?' Angela slurped her tea and wiped her mouth.

'You don't have any friends in Didlinton. So who did you have a curry with?'

'I make friends as I travel around,' Angela said vaguely.

'Oh, never mind. I'm going to bed.'

Poppy got up, irritated already with her mother.

'Want to come with me tomorrow? I've got keys from the estate agent to view a property.'

'I might.' Poppy went upstairs, still fuming.

★ ★ ★

After lunch the next day they walked over to the other side of the village to view the property. Angela had a printout with the details of the house and its location. As they arrived, Poppy realised it was the same estate where Mina Hendry lived. The house was in a different street, parallel to and north of Mina's.

'What do you think?' Angela asked as they both stared at the house.

It was a pebble-dashed semi-detached property like all its neighbours. The paintwork was cream with a blue painted door, and it was a corner property so its garden was bigger. The garden had a privet hedge round it. They couldn't see much inside because of the hedge. The adjoining house looked neat and well-kept too. Its front garden was open with a small oblong of grass and a couple of potted plants.

'It looks nice,' Poppy said. 'Have you got the keys?'

Angela waved them at her with a smile. 'Let's go in.'

The hallway was bright and welcoming and smelled of fresh paint. The walls were magnolia. A steep staircase ran from the hall upstairs. The hall led straight ahead to a kitchen and to the right, there was a door into a living room.

'Is anyone living here?' Poppy asked.

Angela shook her head. 'No, they've moved out into their new house apparently. The furniture that's left is included in the rental price.'

'They've left quite a lot,' Poppy commented.

The living room was a good size and another door off it led to a small dining room. The kitchen looked as if its units had been installed recently and the cooker looked brand new.

'Shall we go upstairs?' Angela said, smiling.

Upstairs, there were two bedrooms and a bathroom. Again, the rooms were a good size.

'What do you think?' Angela asked, sounding slightly anxious.

'It doesn't matter what I think,' Poppy said, shrugging. 'You're the one who'd be living here. Do you like it?'

'I do like it. But do you? I'm hoping you might come and visit me, so I want you to like it as much as I do.'

Poppy was touched that it mattered so much to Angela what she thought. They were standing in the smaller of the two bedrooms.

'This could be your room when you visit,' Angela said.

'It's really nice,' Poppy said, meaning it.

It was a pleasant room with a view out onto the back garden. The owner had obviously been a keen gardener because the garden was full of colourful flowers and shrubs.

'That's good,' Angela said. 'Because I've already rented it.'

'What?'

'I rented the house.' Angela laughed and twirled around. 'It's mine.'

'You should have told me,' Poppy said crossly.

'Oh, you'd only have told me to check for boring things like damp or noisy neighbours. I liked it immediately and I had to have it.'

It was true, Poppy thought. She would have told Angela to check all sorts of things cautiously before agreeing to rent. It would have been sensible but not as much fun as the spontaneity with which her mother lived her life.

Angela began to run from room to room and Poppy followed her. They were laughing like kids as they ran. There was a freedom and a madness that was pure fun.

They ran out into the garden and Angela threw herself down onto the soft grass to lie on her back, her chest rising and falling with exertion. Poppy lay down too and stared at the blue sky. They lay in companionable silence for a while.

'Do you want to talk about it?' Angela murmured.

'About what?' Poppy yawned. Honestly, it was so warm she'd fall asleep if she wasn't careful.

'About your young man, Simon. I saw the postcard. You're missing him.'

'He's not my young man.'

Angela raised herself up on one elbow and looked down into Poppy's face.

'Come on, Poppy. Your dad and I raised you to tell the truth.'

Poppy was going to say that her dad had raised her, not Angela. but she didn't.

'I'm in love with him,' she said. 'But we had an argument and now he's gone. He says it's for a few days, but what if he doesn't come back before I have to go home?'

'Does he know how you feel?'

'No, I didn't know myself until he'd gone. I want to tell him but I can't if he's not here.'

'And does he feel the same way about you?' Angela asked.

'I don't know. I hope so. Harry says he does.'

Angela rolled her eyes.

'Harry's a marvel. He'll be right. He always is. So, what did you argue about?'

'We've been looking into Simon's aunt's death. His mum thinks it wasn't an accident. All of a sudden, Simon wants to stop investigating. I want to keep going. That's the long and the short of it.'

'What a waste of a lovely summer,' Angela said, lying back down. 'Grubbing about in people's lives and writing stuff down in a notebook. When you could be shopping or eating or swimming. Simon's right. Give it up. Pay more attention to your love life and invite him out for drinks.'

'I might have known you wouldn't understand,' Poppy said.

'What are you talking about?'

'It takes planning and dedication and putting in the hours to investigate,'

Poppy said snappily. 'Not qualities that you possess.'

Angela pushed up from her prone position to sit cross-legged on the grass. She looked serious for once.

'I'm not going to let that pass, young lady.'

Poppy made a little sound of impatience but Angela shushed her.

'No, you listen to me. I don't live a conventional life, that's true. I chose to leave you and your Dad so I could travel. I've already admitted I was a rubbish mother. I probably did you a favour by leaving. I'd only have screwed you up.

'But believe it or not, sweetie, it takes planning and dedication and 'putting in the hours' as you put it, to travel successfully and write for journals and make enough cash to live on. Your dad isn't paying for this rental. I am.'

'Fair enough,' Poppy said angrily, 'But how about you show the same dedication to me? You said you were ashamed of how you left me when I was small and how you came back to England to make it up to me. I haven't seen much evidence of that.'

Angela looked upset.

'I thought it was obvious. I've rented this place. That's my proof to you that I love you and that I want us to be closer. I want to try again to be a mum, if you'll let me.'

Poppy's anger disappeared. Angela was trying, in her own way. The house rental meant more than she'd realised.

'OK,' she said finally.

'I want this to work,' Angela said earnestly. 'I really do. I . . . I want to make it different. I can't be the mum you wanted as a young child, but I can be your mum now. Please . . .'

'I can't call you Mum. I never did, even as a child.'

Poppy risked a small smile and saw Angela respond with a smile of her own.

Angela shrugged. 'Fair enough. Shall we go and peek in the cellar and see if it's dark and creepy like in the movies?'

'OK.'

The cellar was disappointingly ordinary with good electric lighting. It had been cleared out and the concrete floor swept clean.

'Lots of storage space,' Angela commented, pointing to the shelves lining the back wall.

'And not a creepy flickering light in the place,' Poppy joked.

Angela laughed.

'I'd like us to be closer,' Poppy said and reached out to hug her.

Angela looked surprised and pleased. She gave Poppy a fierce hug back.

'I'm sorry for everything.'

'When will you move in?'

'Glad to get rid of me?'

Poppy blushed as the thought had crossed her mind. 'No, I'll miss you — but I guess Gilly will be home again before long.'

'Soon. I'll move in soon. You can help me. I don't have much stuff but I have some in storage at your dad's so I'll need to get that sent down.'

'Does Dad know you've rented a

264

house?'

'I wanted to tell you first. We can tell him together. Phone him tonight?'

Angela slung her arm through Poppy's as they walked home. They chatted easily. It felt like the beginning of their new relationship and it helped her forget about Simon for a while. She hoped he was happy at his parents' and that he'd be back quickly.

Gilly's cottage smelled of cigarette smoke instead of lavender. Poppy waved the smell away.

'That's it. You're forbidden from smoking in the house. It stinks.'

'Aha. I knew you'd say that eventually, so I got one of these.' Angela rummaged in her bag and came up with a glass and metal contraption. After a few minutes she inhaled in delight. A sweet scent of strawberry and watermelon wafted up into Poppy's nose.

Something clicked in her brain. She'd smelled this before. Twice.

She spun round to face Angela.

'I know who killed Mary Soull.'

15

'You can't just barge in there and accuse her,' Angela argued, as she and Poppy paced the small living room.

'I smelled that scent of watermelon and strawberry the first evening I arrived in Didlinton and saw someone watching Simon's home. I smelled it again in Mina Hendry's house. At the time I thought it was over-ripe fruit but now I'm sure it's those flavours from an e-cigarette.'

'It could be a coincidence,' Angela said.

'I don't think so. That's why I need to go over there and confront her. I'll know by her face if she's telling the truth.'

'I don't like it. You could get hurt.'

Poppy could tell she wasn't going to get away easily unless she included Angela. Her concern radiated from her and she was biting her nails.

'She's not going to attack me,' Poppy said, with more confidence than she felt.

She remembered how tall and broad Mina Hendry was. She was bigger than most women in build. She could easily have overpowered Mary Soull, Poppy thought. Photos of Mary which Simon had shown her showed a slight figure of about average height, like Poppy's own size.

'You can come with me,' she said to Angela. 'That way, you'll be reassured that I'm fine.'

'You're not going right now?' Angela said, sounding shocked.

'I am going now. There's no reason to wait, is there? Come on, let's get our jackets in case it gets cold, and we'll walk over.'

As they walked over to the estate on the other side of the village, Poppy laid out her plan. It was a simple one. She would go to the front door in the normal manner and hopefully be invited inside where she would talk to Mina. In the meantime, Angela would sneak into the Hendrys' back garden and keep watch for any trouble. She had her mobile phone and told Poppy she wasn't afraid to use it to call the police if necessary.

'I'll try to get Mina to take me to the kitchen to talk,' Poppy said. 'That way, you'll hopefully see us and can keep an eye on me. We're probably being too cautious. She's an older woman, what harm can she do me?'

'If she killed her best friend, then the answer to that is quite a lot!'

Poppy looked at her mother.

'This is insane, isn't it? What if I'm wrong?'

'What if you're right?'

★ ★ ★

Mina Hendry's front door looked as innocuous as the others in the street. It was evening and most people were probably having their evening meal because there was no one around.

A few abandoned kids' bicycles and scooters lay on the pavement and a football was on the road. Poppy kicked it back onto the pavement so its owner could find it safely.

'Why would she kill Mary?' Angela said.

'I have no idea. That's what I'm here to find out.' Poppy stared at the house, looking for any sign of life. 'Maybe she's not in.'

She sort of hoped that was the case. She wasn't scared exactly, but she was nervous. And on the edge of being embarrassed. It was a monstrous accusation to make to anyone.

What if Mina laughed at her? What if she denied everything and made Poppy look like a fool? Worse, what if she was angry and called the police and accused Poppy of harassment? She was on the verge of calling it all off when Angela darted away and disappeared up the side street.

Taking a deep breath, Poppy walked up the short path to the front door and rang the bell. There was a long pause before she heard someone coming. Her palms were damp and her heartbeat raced along to its own tune. She tried to calm down. She didn't want to look suspicious. She tucked her hair behind her ears and plastered on a smile.

The door opened and Mina Hendry stood there, frowning. She didn't seem to recognise Poppy.

'Yes?'

'Hello, Mrs Hendry. I'm Poppy. I came to see you with Simon, Mary's nephew. Can I come in for a moment?'

'I don't know. I'm not well . . .' Mina said.

Her hair was lank and the grooves from her nose to her mouth were like deep cuts in her pale complexion. She was wearing an old-fashioned house coat over a long corduroy skirt and her feet were encased in leather shoes that had seen better days.

'I'm sorry to hear that, but this will only take a few minutes,' Poppy said with her brightest smile.

Mina let out an audible sigh and stepped back.

'Very well, if you must. Come in. You'll have to make do with a seat in my kitchen, I'm afraid. I've been lying down in the living room and it's a mess so I can't take a visitor in there.'

Perfect, thought Poppy. *That's just where I want to be.* She hoped that Angela was hiding out of sight.

'Is it flu?' she asked.

'What? Oh, no, I get these migraines. I've been in the living room for the past three days with the curtains drawn. I'm feeling a bit better now.'

'I'm glad you're on the mend,' Poppy said politely.

She stopped short. On the wall behind the front door was a coat rack. There was a large white jacket and hat perched on one of the brass hooks. She'd seen them before at the bird watching excursion. The rude man who had shushed her as they went into the woods had worn them.

Mina went into the kitchen and sat heavily on one of the oak chairs. Poppy tried to glance out at the back garden without making it obvious. All she saw was the green grass of the lawn and the herbaceous borders. There was a shed at the far left hand corner and she wondered if Angela was hiding behind it.

'Cup of tea?' Mina offered, sounding tired.

'Shall I make it?' Poppy offered.

Mina grunted and she took that as an affirmative. The kettle was full and warm to the touch so she pressed the switch to boil it up. Mina told her where the teabags and mugs were kept. Poppy was aware of her gaze on her back as she made the tea. It felt like a hot prickling between her shoulder blades. She was very aware of the other woman's height and strength as she turned back with two mugs.

'Is your husband in?' Poppy asked, casually.

'What's that got to do with you?' Mina said, her eyes narrowing.

'Sorry, I didn't mean to be nosy,' Poppy said, 'It's just that I think I might have met him at a recent bird watching outing.'

Mina's expression darkened. 'It wouldn't surprise me. He's out and about at all hours with his birds. And not a care for me, sitting in here bored to death. I've had to get my own meals these last three days despite being ill. Where's he been? Out watching some stupid birds nesting in the woods.'

Poppy sipped her tea, uncertain how to begin. How did one accuse someone of murder in their own home over a nice cup of tea? She wished that Simon was here. He was better at talking calmly to people and he was taller and stronger than her or Mina.

Actually, she wished Simon was here because she was in love with him. She missed his smile, his dimple and his lovely intense blue eyes. She was lost for a moment in thoughts of him until a noise from Mina brought her back. She was smacking her lips angrily over her husband.

'You might remember that Simon and I were asking about his aunt Mary's tragic death,' Poppy said.

'I'm not senile,' Mina said nastily. 'Of course I remember. I told you to check out that actor from *Heaven's Harvest*.'

'Yes, that's right.'

Poppy realised how cleverly Mina had deflected them. Firstly, she'd told them about Brandon Tulloe and when that didn't work, she'd told them about Liz Soames. She was trying to put them off the trail that led right back to her.

'Did you check him out?' Mina said.

'We did but he had an alibi. Just as Liz Soames did.'

'It was an accident anyway. The police said so. Why are you stirring things up?' Mina looked angry.

'We convinced ourselves it was an accident too,' Poppy said, 'But then someone broke into Simon's home, clearly looking for something. The same person was watching his cottage. That's a sign of a guilty conscience. That person has something to hide. And I know who it is.'

'You don't know anything. You're lying. I want you to leave now.'

Mina got up from her chair, staring at Poppy, her face reddened and eyebrows knitted together. Her fists were clenched and Poppy felt a first shiver of fear.

Don't be ridiculous, she thought to herself. She was in a ordinary semi-detached house, in an everyday kitchen. Nothing bad could happen.

'Why do you want me to leave?' she said bravely. 'Have you got something to hide? Why did you kill Mary Soull?'

Poppy was on the tips of her toes, ready to flee if Mina launched across the table to get to her. A variety of emotions flitted across Mina's face until she plummeted down onto her chair and burst into loud sobbing. It was like the wailing of a child, complete and abandoned with no notion of propriety.

Poppy didn't know what to do. She searched in her pocket for a clean handkerchief and came up empty. She got up and grabbed the roll of kitchen towelling beside the kettle on a wooden holder. She tore off a piece and pushed it towards the older woman. She hadn't expected tears. She'd expected either a vehement denial or to have to make a run for it.

Mina's face was hidden. Her large, bony hands supported her head and her elbows were on the surface of the oak table. Her greasy hair was thin and showed her scalp. Poppy felt an unwelcome twinge of compassion. If Mina had killed Mary, she didn't deserve Poppy's sympathy. But she was a pitiful sight right now.

She waited. A series of loud sobs resonated in the room. She looked out the window but there was no sign of Angela. Eventually the sobs subsided and Mina took ragged gulps of air and hiccupped. She raised a ruined face to Poppy. Her eyes were bloodshot, her cheeks pink with broken veins and her open mouth revealed uneven, yellowed teeth.

'Vincent is never here. As I said, he's always somewhere bird watching. I've tried to get used to it. Liz Soames once joked that I was a bird watching widow. Revolting woman. But I can accept that. I have accepted it. But Mary was a different matter. She was my friend, not his. We'd have coffee or lunch, you know? If

I needed a natter, she was there. Then suddenly she wasn't. She made excuses or she didn't pick up the phone when I called. She was out. With *him*. With my husband.

'She was going to visit her sister on that Monday. She at least had the decency to let me know that beforehand. I'd picked up the courage to talk to her about it. About Vincent and being with him so much. That it wasn't right, her being with another woman's husband so much. So, I sent her a text using Vincent's phone. I pretended it was him, wanting to meet. I thought she'd message back to say she was on the train but no. She was willing to meet him to hear what he had to say. She didn't suspect it was me.'

Mina gulped. Her gaze was unfocussed as if she was seeing something else on a far horizon, not Poppy who was glued to her seat listening.

'You met her on the cliff path . . .' Poppy whispered, unwilling to break the spell.

'I asked her to meet me, or rather

Vincent, at the cliff path. I knew from Vincent that's where he went to view the sea birds on the sea stacks. There's a small path and a bench where he used to sit and use his telescope. I'd never been up there but it wasn't hard to find. I got there first and waited for her.

I was angry. It was all boiling up inside me. I was jealous of them and I was sure they were having an affair. I couldn't believe it was all just about those silly birds. There had to be more to it. I wasn't going to let Mary steal my Vincent away from me. We've been married for forty years.

She was surprised to see me there. She was all dressed up for the bird watching. She had a wide-brimmed hat and her binoculars and solid walking boots. She asked me why I was there and where was Vincent. When she said his name, I saw red. We argued. I accused her of having an affair with him and do you know what she did?'

Mina looked at Poppy, focussed properly now. Her fingers clenched and

278

unclenched on the table top in agitation.

'What did she do, Mina?' Poppy asked.

'She laughed at me,' Mina cried out. 'How dare she! All that worry I had and the sleepless nights mulling it over and all she did was laugh. She called me a silly old fool. Well, I couldn't let that pass, could I? I took her by her shoulders and I shook her hard. She wasn't laughing then. Somehow . . . I can't explain it . . . we were on the edge of the path and it was slippery even though it hadn't rained and her foot . . . it went over the grass lip . . . and then she teetered. I tried to grab her but it was too late, she'd gone.'

Poppy felt sick. Mina moaned and wiped her mouth. Her large hands were shaking. Poppy imagined them on Mary's fragile shoulders, shaking and shaking.

'It was a horrible accident,' Mina said. 'She was gone and there was nothing I could do about it. It wasn't going to make it any better if I went to the police. So I kept quiet. I walked home and I made a cup of tea and one of my headaches came on so I went to bed for the rest of the day.'

'It was you watching Simon's cottage, wasn't it?' Poppy said. 'And you broke in and went through his stuff.'

'I had to know if he suspected anything. I'd been watching the cottage on and off for a while until you showed up and nearly caught me. I realised I had to stop doing that. I didn't break in to his home, he'd left the door unlocked. By that stage, you'd been asking questions and I wanted to know what you'd found out. I didn't find anything of use.'

'Does Vincent know?'

Mina shook her head. 'I didn't tell him what happened. You know what's funny?'

She didn't wait for Poppy to answer before continuing. 'He's out more than ever since Mary died. I thought she was stealing him away but now I hardly see him at all.' She laughed and Poppy winced. It was a harsh and humourless sound.

There was a crash from the garden and

they both were startled. Outside, Poppy saw the shrubs shaking violently and heard raised voices. The next moment the back door into the kitchen opened and Angela stumbled in, followed by an older, irate man.

'I found this person skulking in our back garden,' he bellowed.

Poppy realised it was the old man from the excursion, minus his distinctive white jacket and hat. His eyes widened in recognition as he took in Poppy sitting opposite his wife. He pushed Angela into a chair. She had twigs and leaves in her hair and she looked worried.

'What's going on?' he shouted. 'If I don't get answers, I'm calling the police.'

'Tie them up,' Mina cried, standing up, 'Get a rope, Vincent. They're intruders in our house.'

Angela screamed and Poppy felt sick again. This was all going horribly wrong.

'I dropped my phone,' Angela cried out to Poppy. 'We can't get help.'

Mina lunged towards Angela and Poppy leaped at her to prevent her touching her mother. Vincent was bawling and waving the landline phone and threatening all sorts. To add to the confusion, another person dashed in through the open back door and began shouting in a loud voice.

It was Simon.

Poppy was so relieved to see him. She'd never heard Simon raise his voice before. His voice was louder than all the other cries and shouts in the room. When he slammed his fist down on the table it shut everyone up for an instant.

'That's better,' he said. 'Mr Hendry, please sit down. Mrs Hendry, please let go of Angela's shirt collar and sit down. Poppy, close your mouth, it's hanging open. Angela, well done.'

'Well done? What did you do?' Poppy asked.

'I left a message for Harry to tell him where we'd gone. I didn't want us to disappear and no one would know,' Angela grinned.

'That was a bit dramatic,' Poppy teased weakly.

She was only half joking. She was very glad that her mother had left a message and that somehow and wonderfully Simon had picked that message up and come and rescued them.

His arrival and taking charge — evidently honed through years spent taming unruly classes of pupils — had calmed the situation down. Mina had collapsed in on herself, her chin resting on her chest and her breathing deep and uneven. Vincent looked confused. Angela looked happy and as for Poppy — well, she didn't know how she looked, but inside her a choir was singing love songs.

'The police are on their way,' Simon announced. 'We'll sit here calmly until they get here.'

'The police? What's it all about?' Vincent Hendry asked, bewildered.

'Ask your wife,' Poppy said gently.

Mina groaned but didn't move. Vincent put out a shaky hand and touched her shoulder.

'Mina, dear?'

Simon sat beside Poppy. He smiled

tentatively at her. 'Are you OK?'

Poppy smiled back. 'Why are you here? Aren't you meant to be at your parents'?'

'I missed you so I came back early. We need to talk.'

'I missed you too,' Poppy murmured, her heart swelling with joy.

★ ★ ★

The police arrived shortly afterwards and they had to go to the station to make statements. They were allowed away after that and having left their details, were told they may be called upon further.

Angela announced that she was going to the shops to get some celebratory food. Poppy and Simon walked slowly home together.

'Do you think she murdered Mary, or was it an accident as she claims?' Poppy said.

Simon shook his head.

'I guess we'll never know for sure. I feel sorry for Mr Hendry. He hadn't a clue about any of it.'

'Maybe it's wrong but I feel sorry for Mina as well,' Poppy said. 'She's a victim too, in a way.'

'People are complicated,' Simon remarked.

Poppy leaned against him.

'So, you missed me?'

'I missed you so much I had to come back early. Mum wasn't pleased but she cheered up when I said I'd bring you to visit them.'

'So, how much did you miss me?' Poppy persisted.

'This much,' Simon said and took a gentle hold of her chin, tipping it up so that when he leaned down, his mouth met hers.

'Mmm,' Poppy said, when they came up for air. 'I'm not terribly convinced, I'm afraid. Show me again.'

'You're very demanding, but if you insist.'

Some time later, Poppy murmured, 'Is this a summer romance, do you think?'

'Let's wait and see. It's whatever we want it to be.'

They went into Gilly's cottage. Harry was there and was relieved to see them. Angela arrived back with a chicken and vegetables. They made a meal and described to Harry all that had occurred.

Some time later, Poppy scraped the last bit of chicken from her plate and patted her stomach in contentment.

The cats were sitting in a row, eyes fixed on the chicken carcass. Harry put a few slices on a plate and set it on the floor, where they tolerated each other long enough to eat it.

It felt like an ending, Poppy thought. They'd solved the mystery of Mary Soull's death. But it felt like a possible beginning too as she looked at her companions. Harry and Angela were laughing over a joke Harry had told. Simon was looking back at her with a smile.

'Dessert?' Angela called, and they all raised their spoons in agreement.

16

There were thirty bright little faces turned in her direction. Poppy felt the stiff newness of her dress and tights, her blue shoes pinching at her heels as she stood in front of her class.

No more casual tees and shorts. No more sun cream and no more beach. Outside the classroom, it was raining. Sheets of the stuff coming down with a dull metal sky beyond.

'I want you to write me a story,' she said. 'The title is *What I Did In My Summer Holidays* and when you've written it, I want you to draw me a lovely picture to go with it.'

There was a sheet of lined paper in front of each of her pupils and a big sheet of sugar paper for a picture. Soon, there were bent heads and concentrated expressions and a few squabbles over colouring pens, which Poppy sorted out using her years of experience teaching eight-year-olds.

What I did in my summer holidays, she mused, sitting at her teacher's desk and marking the arithmetic jotters from that morning. *Imagine what I could write and draw about mine. There was all the excitement of the sleuthing and then there was Simon.*

But she mustn't think about him. It was too confusing. In the end, it had been a summer romance. Now, she had to put all that behind her and get on with her life.

The problem was, she wasn't sure what she wanted from her life any more. She'd always loved working here in the primary school in Edinburgh with her flat just up the road and her father's home a ten-minute walk further on. Now, she wondered if she might travel, as all her friends did so casually. She might buy a large canvas rucksack from the hiking shop on the high street, fill it with essentials and off she'd go.

She'd need to renew her passport, of course. And she'd need to decide where to go. Perhaps she'd teach abroad. They were always looking for teachers, and as an English speaker she'd be in demand.

China was very far away. That was a possibility. The problem was that wherever she went, she'd still miss Simon.

She stared at the jotter in front of her and the pen in her fingers. She hadn't marked a single sum in it. This wouldn't do. She had to move on, as Simon had done. He had moved to Didlinton and accepted a temporary teaching post in the local school. He hoped it'd be made permanent as there were a couple of retirements coming up.

He had told her this on the evening of Angela's housewarming. That evening as they'd celebrated escaping from the Hendrys' house and solving the mystery of Mary's death, Angela had announced she was moving in to her new home.

'It's fast, I know,' she said, over a dessert of crushed strawberries, double cream and meringues. 'But the owners are abroad, they wanted someone in the property quickly and the paperwork is all going through. There's nothing to stop me moving in, and I have no belongings except what's in storage in Edinburgh. I'll ask John to arrange to send it down. We should have a housewarming party.'

'Jolly good idea,' Harry said. 'I'll bring a fish to grill.'

'That's sorted, then.' Angela clapped her hands enthusiastically. 'Put it in your diary, folks.'

* * *

The evening of Angela's house party was warm and sunny. It was the peak of the summer and the days were long. Poppy could never make her mind up whether she liked spring or summer best. Spring was lovely with baby lambs and daffodils and the promise of summer still to come, but summer when it came was simply perfect. Hot sunshine, long bright evenings and holidays.

The doors of Angela's new home were wide open and music wafted out along with chatter and laughter. She had wisely invited her new neighbours so there were no complaints about noise. The house was still sparsely furnished with whatever the owners had left. Poppy knew that her mother was sleeping in a sleeping bag in the main upstairs bedroom because her new bed and mattress hadn't yet been delivered.

'It's the best time to hold a party,' Angela had told her. 'It means no one can wreck your belongings because there aren't any.'

The guests had been generous, bringing food and drink with them. Angela had bought a huge mountain of snacks which was laid out on the kitchen table as a buffet for people to help themselves. Harry had been as good as his word and provided freshly caught fish, which he was currently grilling to add to the feast. Simon had contributed bottles of wine and Poppy had brought a decent supply of sweets and chocolates.

Gilly had returned home as she always did, a week before Poppy headed north so that they could share their summer stories. This year, Poppy's story outdid Gilly's by far.

'I can't believe it,' Gilly kept saying. 'Tell me again about Mina and how you worked it all out.'

Poppy took her glass of lemonade and went outside, amazed at how many friends Angela had acquired locally. Some people had invited themselves. She recognised a few of the cast of *Heaven's Harvest*. Tabby waved to her. She was sitting on the lawn with Sam and Gordie. Liz Soames was talking to Jean and Shirley from the bird watching club, over in a cluster of plastic garden chairs that someone had lent Angela for the party. Derek and his wife were not present.

Michael Carmody, dressed quite formally in cream trousers and a green jumper, came over to speak to her, leaving a pretty woman with neat blonde hair and stylish dress.

'It's quite a party,' he said. 'Thanks for the invitation. Hilda and I are enjoying ourselves.'

'It was the least we could do after our behaviour,' Poppy said.

'I was sorry to hear about Vincent and his wife. Vincent didn't deserve that.'

'How is he?'

'I haven't seen him but the house is up for sale. I saw that when I was on my way here.'

'I almost wish we hadn't meddled,' Poppy said.

'The truth must come out. That's important,' Michael stated, in his bombastic way. 'Now, excuse me, Hilda's waiting for me. All the best.'

Poppy went inside. Where was Simon? It was almost as if he was avoiding her. She went to the kitchen where Harry was serving up grilled fish fillets. There was a rhubarb sauce to go with them and he was dishing it up with lavish dollops.

'Fish?' he shouted at her, over the hubbub.

'Have you seen Simon?' she called back.

'No sign of him. Don't think he's arrived yet.'

Poppy wandered back out and into the living room. Angela was holding court with a circle of friends, none of whom she knew, except for Gilly. Then there was a tap on her shoulder. She turned, expecting it to be Simon, but it wasn't.

'Dad, what on earth are you doing here?' She threw her arms round him and hugged him tightly.

'I heard there was a party so I flew down.'

'You flew?' Poppy raised her eyebrows.

'Yes, not very environmentally friendly, I know. But I can't miss your mother's housewarming. She rented an entire house, for goodness' sake. She's finally putting down her roots.'

Poppy touched his arm. 'We don't know if she'll stay for good. Don't get your hopes up.'

'Darling, are you talking to me or to you?' John said gently. 'We both know what your mother is like. We'll never know for certain when she'll leap up and vanish overseas. The difference is that now she has her own place to return to, if she wants to keep it on. Angela's not daft. She's getting older and she needs this.'

'What about you, Dad? What do you need?' Poppy asked with concern.

She felt protective of him. She always had. It had been the two of them against the world when she was younger.

'I never stopped loving her,' he said. 'I'm too old to stop now. And I accepted, a very long time ago, what she's like. It's part of the reason I love her. She's spontaneous and free and creative. All the things that I'm not. She complements me, if you like.'

'I don't want you to get hurt.'

John hugged her tightly. 'You're my best girl, Poppy, and I love you — but you need to find what you need. Let me decide what I need. I'm not going to get hurt. I've got a thicker hide than you realise.'

'John!' Angela broke through her circle of listeners and ran towards them. 'You made it. I wasn't sure you'd come.'

Poppy stood aside as her parents

embraced. She saw now the fondness between them. It had always been there — it was an unconventional relationship but it suited them.

She saw Angela kiss her father on the cheek and whisper something in his ear. He chuckled. Poppy left them to it. She had to find Simon.

He was just coming into the house.

'Sorry I'm late,' he said, seeing her. 'I had an important phone call to take.'

'Sounds super mysterious,' she joked, pleased to see him.

'Shall we find a place to talk?' He wasn't smiling and his whole demeanour was stiff.

'Is everything OK?' she asked.

'Of course. It's just so busy in here, I can hardly think let alone speak.'

'Shall we go upstairs?' Poppy suggested, then blushed. 'I meant, I have the second bedroom and it's quiet up there. We can chat.'

Angela had been as good as her word and offered Poppy the smaller upstairs room as her own for whenever she visited. There was no furniture in it and no curtains, but she had put in a couple of large floor cushions and an old coffee table from a charity shop in the meantime.

Poppy felt unexpectedly awkward as she led the way to her room. Simon was in a strange mood, hardly a party mood. They had been dating since he kissed her that day at Mina Hendry's. Neither of them had spoken about the future. By silent agreement they had concentrated on enjoying the summer with walks along the beach, meals by candlelight and day trips along the coast to interesting sites.

'I had a phone call with the head teacher at the local school,' Simon said, sitting on one of the floor cushions, his long legs stuck out in front of him. 'They've offered me a teaching post beginning when the schools go back.'

'That's wonderful,' Poppy said, tucking her feet in under her on the other cushion.

'It's temporary but there's a possibility

of extension,' he said.

'Well, you're sorted,' she said lightly. 'You've got a home and a job in Didlinton. That's fantastic.'

'Yes, I'm pleased,' he said, sounding anything but pleased.

'What is it? What's the matter?'

'We've had a great summer . . .' Simon said slowly. His gaze was on his hands.

'Hey, summer's still on. We're *having* a great summer,' Poppy said brightly, though her heart was sinking. What was he going to say? She dreaded it.

'What we said the other evening . . .'

'You mean when we stood under the stars on the beach and I said I was in love with you and you said you loved me too?'

'Yes. That.'

'What are you saying? That it isn't true? That you don't love me?' Poppy said. Her throat felt dry.

'It's complicated,' Simon said, sounding wretched.

At last his gaze met hers. She was struck, as usual, by the intensity of his

298

blue eyes. She loved him so much, and she felt as if she was losing him. And she didn't know why.

'How can it be complicated?' she said desperately. 'We love each other. Isn't that enough?'

'I love you, Poppy. But I've only stopped loving Suzie recently. I haven't given myself time to get over that and . . . *find* myself. I need to do that first before I can commit to you. Do you understand?'

'No, I don't understand. But I respect your decision. I can't force you to want me.'

She could hardly see him through the blur of her tears. He reached for her but she drew back.

'Don't try to comfort me when you've caused this. Please leave.'

'Poppy . . .'

'Just leave,' she shouted, finishing with a sob.

She kept her eyes shut until he'd gone. She stayed in her bedroom while the party boomed below and the floorboards seemed to vibrate with music and laughter and fun. She curled up on the floor cushion and wanted to sleep, to hide from the world.

Angela found her there much later when the party was over.

'It's all right,' she soothed as Poppy wept. 'Give him space, sweetie and he'll realise how much he loves you. It's better to let it take its course and then he'll know what's right. Come downstairs now. Your dad and I are going to watch a film.'

'You haven't got a telly,' Poppy sniffed, rubbing her wet eyes.

'We've got a laptop and we can squash up. Come along and spend a quiet evening with your old parents. It'll do you good.'

★ ★ ★

It did do her good. The three of them squished up against each other on the couch, with Angela's laptop on her knee and her and Dad craning their necks to see the screen properly. She didn't follow the plot much and couldn't have told who the main characters were afterwards, but by the end of the film she knew she was going home.

And here she was now. Back at work in Edinburgh with the rain pouring down and lots of eager children showing her pictures of sand and sea and some other, more exotic locations. They ranged from days out at Portobello Beach to a stay at Granny's on Arran to Cindy Martin's trip to Dubai and a camel ride at dusk.

'Put your pens away tidily and then sit with your arms folded nicely until the bell rings. The first table ready gets to go out the door first.'

There was a bit of a scramble and the noise level rose, but Poppy didn't intervene. It was Friday afternoon after all.

She thought about her lonely weekend ahead. She'd been invited out for drinks by her friends but she didn't like it. The forecast was for rain both days. Her dad was down in Didlinton visiting Angela, as he did with increasing frequency. He'd told her he might sell up his home in Edinburgh and move down to be near her mother. Angela had suggested it, and Gilly thought it a wonderful idea.

The pupils vanished in a scampering of feet, leaving an empty classroom with the usual forgotten satchel, lunchbox and someone's spare gym shoes.

Poppy put on her raincoat and picked up her bag. She returned goodbyes and wishes for a great weekend as she went through the hall and out of the door.

★ ★ ★

There was a tall man standing outside the gates of the school. He looked at Poppy with familiar blue eyes and as he smiled, a dimple appeared in his right cheek.

She ran to him and Simon kissed her deeply.

'I'm ready — and thank you for

waiting for me to sort myself out,' he said simply. 'I love you, Poppy Johnson. Will you marry me?'

We do hope that you have enjoyed reading this large print book.

Did you know that all of our titles are available for purchase?

We publish a wide range of high quality large print books including:
Romances, Mysteries, Classics
General Fiction
Non Fiction and Westerns

Special interest titles available in large print are:
The Little Oxford Dictionary
Music Book, Song Book
Hymn Book, Service Book

Also available from us courtesy of Oxford University Press:
Young Readers' Dictionary
(large print edition)
Young Readers' Thesaurus
(large print edition)

For further information or a free brochure, please contact us at:
Ulverscroft Large Print Books Ltd.,
The Green, Bradgate Road, Anstey,
Leicester, LE7 7FU, England.
Tel: (00 44) 0116 236 4325
Fax: (00 44) 0116 234 0205

Other titles in the
Linford Romance Library:

WRONG PATHS

Gail Richards

Nicola hasn't always chosen the right path. But now, having left her job and her last boyfriend, she's trying to get back on track. Scraping the gorgeous Joel Walker's car in a country lane isn't a great start, though! As she gets drawn into his life, she realises he's shadowed by mystery, corruption and murder. Is this yet another wrong path for Nicola? Will Joel bring danger — or the romance she's been hoping for all her life?